-X-

W9-BWZ-501

JUSTICE AT REDWILLOW

JUSTICE AT REDWILLOW

JOHN D. NESBITT

FIVE STAR
A part of Gale, Cengage Learning

GALE
CENGAGE Learning·

Farmington Hills, Mich • San Francisco • New York • Waterville, Maine
Meriden, Conn • Mason, Ohio • Chicago

GALE
CENGAGE Learning·

LIBRARY OF CONGRESS CATALOGING-IN-PUBLICATION DATA

Nesbitt, John D.
    Justice at Redwillow / John D. Nesbitt. — First edition.
        pages ; cm
    ISBN 978-1-4328-3049-6 (hardcover) — ISBN 1-4328-3049-X (hardcover) — ISBN 978-1-4328-3046-5 (ebook) — ISBN 1-4328-3046-5 (ebook)
        1. Ranchers—Fiction. 2. Murder—Investigation—Fiction. 3. Revenge—Fiction. I. Title.
    PS3564.E76J87 2015
    813'.54—dc23   2015008342

First Edition. First Printing: August 2015
Find us on Facebook– https://www.facebook.com/FiveStarCengage
Visit our website– http://www.gale.cengage.com/fivestar/
Contact Five Star™ Publishing at FiveStar@cengage.com

Printed in the United States of America
1 2 3 4 5 6 7 19 18 17 16 15

for Trey Fortune

CHAPTER ONE

Fontaine gave one last tug on the cinch and untied his horse from the wagon wheel. He led the buckskin out on a half-circle, came to a stop, and checked the cinch. He was still getting to know the horse, and he had a long ride ahead. The girth was tight, so Fontaine led the animal back to the wagon.

Old Ben Spoonhammer stood by the tailgate, tugging at a pair of grey leather gloves. "All set?"

"I guess so." Fontaine came to a stop.

"Well, I wish you all the best."

"Same to you, Ben."

"You should find it plumb easy." The old man waved his gloved hand to the north. "You can see those buttes from ten miles away, and with that map, there'll be no mistake about which parcel's yours."

"I'm sure there won't be any question."

Ben's eyes sparkled as his bearded face turned into a smile. "Well, give 'er hell." He pulled the glove off his right hand and reached forward to shake.

Fontaine stepped ahead of the horse and held out his hand. As the two men shook, he said, "Same to you, partner. I hope you find what you're looking for."

"Shouldn't be too hard. You grow up with a name like mine, you'd think it had been waitin' for you all this time."

"Like a good little woman."

"Maybe not quite like that, but somewhat similar. There's a

7

place I've got in mind, and if the fella still wants to sell it, I plan to change its name. Call it the Good River Café."

Fontaine raised his eyebrows. He had worked with Ben Spoonhammer all winter, hunting coyotes and then picking up bones, and this was the first time the old man had put a name on what he hoped to do. Fontaine waved toward the south. "Well, whenever I get back to Cheyenne, I'll look for you."

"You do that. And meanwhile, I hope things work out well for you on that little piece of land."

"Thanks." He paused. "I know I've said it before, but I hope having my own place helps me get a new start. And I appreciate your part in it."

"Like I heard in a song once, every river flows to the sea. We're at different points on ours, but we've done all right together. So good luck, partner." The old man smiled again.

"And the same to you." Fontaine set his reins in place and swung aboard. "So long."

The buckskin set out on a fast walk, and Fontaine reached forward to pat its neck. Then he turned to wave at old Ben Spoonhammer, who stood in his battered hat and sagging clothes at the tail end of a wagon in the middle of a spreading grassland.

A hundred yards beyond the old man, a pile of dull bones caught the glare of the sun. It was the last of many piles of antlers, hooves, and bones—mostly bones—all dry, some grey and some white, that the two men had gathered as the country came out of winter. Now it was spring. New grass was pushing through to give a speckled background to the man, the wagon, and the pile of bones.

Fontaine settled in for the long ride, at least two days by the old man's reckoning. A country of muted green stretched away to the north, with sand-colored bluffs rising at liberal distances from one another. Dark spots appeared in draws and side canyons where trees had taken hold.

Grass flowed beneath the hooves of the buckskin. Parts of a song ran through Fontaine's mind, lilting words about a river flowing to the sea. He raised his head as he nudged the horse into a lope, and the breeze felt cool and fresh in his face.

Season of mists. Beads of moisture hung on the prairie grass, and the Dunstan Buttes were shrouded in thin fog. They had not been visible until Fontaine came within a couple of miles. To avoid mistakes, he took out the map that Ben Spoonhammer had given him with the deed and bill of sale.

He found the cabin, set against a hillside facing north. A stocky cedar tree no more than eight feet tall grew on the edge of the shallow draw a few yards west of the cabin. The only other tree on the hundred-and-sixty-acre claim was a dead snag about fifty yards to the northwest. It wasn't much taller than the cedar tree, and all the bark had fallen away. In the quiet, misty morning, with its skeletal branches and an indefinite background, the tree reminded Fontaine of a graveyard.

He swung down from the horse and loosened the cinch. This was camp. More than that, it was his own place. When the weather cleared off, he would get his bearings. For right now he could unload his gear and tie the horse to the dead tree. He picked at the leather strings that tied his bundle to the back of the saddle.

No hurry about anything. He unrolled the canvas sheet on the ground, set his duffel bag and blankets at one end, and slid the saddle off the horse and onto the other end of the canvas. He left the blanket and pad, damp side up, to cover the saddle and air out. After switching the bridle and reins for a halter and rope, he led the buckskin to the old tree. The trunk was about five inches thick where he grabbed it, and the tree did not budge when he shook it. He picketed the horse to the base of the tree and laid the slack on the ground. The horse went to grazing, its buff-colored coat and dark mane set off against the dead grey of the tree.

As Fontaine watched without thinking about anything in particular, he saw the mix of old and new grass, and he noted that the grass was not shaggy with last year's growth but had been grazed off. He figured it was normal for an unfenced claim that no one had looked after. At least the horse had something to eat.

Now for the cabin. No telling what shape it was in. Fontaine pulled the stick out of the hasp and pushed the door open. A blue-black wasp fell on the floor in front of him, so he stepped on the insect and gave his boot sole a turn, ridging the dust on the wooden floor.

The cabin consisted of a single room, about twelve feet by sixteen, and the interior was murky. The room had only one small window on the east, and the glass had a film of dirt and flyspeck. Dust lay on everything—the board shelves, the wires that hung down from the rafters, the table and two rickety chairs, the sheet-iron stove. Cobwebs sagged with dust. News-papers had been tucked between the studs of the board walls, and when Fontaine pecked a finger on one sheet of paper, a small shower of dust fell on his fingernail. Along the bottoms of the walls, mice had chewed away at the papers. Beneath the bunk that was built into the southeast corner of the room, Fontaine found a puffy mouse nest, uninhabited. He rose up and stood back. It was all going to take some cleaning, that was for sure. He figured it was what he could expect when he went from being a bone-hunter to a homesteader. He winced. Now that he thought of it, people like him were called nesters.

The weather cleared off, and the next day was sunny with blue skies. Fontaine had gotten the cabin cleaned and had moved his belongings inside when he heard the nicker of his horse. He walked outside to the far edge of the shallow draw where he could get a better view. Two riders were headed his way from the southwest. When they were within a quarter of a mile, Fontaine could see that each man had a rope tied onto the right side of his saddle and a rifle and scabbard on the left side.

He stood and waited as they rode onto his property and sauntered forward into what was more or less his yard.

"Mornin'," he said.

The two riders muttered a greeting. Then the one on Fontaine's left spoke. "Whose place are you on?"

"My own."

"Is that right?"

"Yep. I bought it from a fella named Ben Spoonhammer."

"Don't know him."

"I don't think he ever stayed here very long, and it would have been awhile back."

"Last I heard, it was owned by a man named March, and that was a long time ago."

"That may be, but Spoonhammer had clear title to it, and I got it from him." Fontaine put on a smile. "Light and set, fellas. I take it you're neighbors?"

Neither man answered, and they made slow work of getting off their horses. As they walked forward leading their mounts, they looked around on the ground. For a moment they reminded Fontaine of tenderfeet on the lookout for snakes.

"My name's Jim Fontaine."

The man who had spoken earlier said, "I'm Fred Barrett." He was a short man, compact and round-muscled, with a short neck. He wore a narrow-brimmed hat that was somewhere between black and brown, and he did not wear a bandanna. His vest was the same color as his hat, as were his holster and his boots. An ivory-handled revolver jutted out of his holster, and large-roweled spurs hung on his boots. As he held his hand forward, he locked his eyes on Fontaine. "Glad to meet you," he said, in a tone that dared a person not to believe him.

When the handshake was over, he stepped back and spit to the side, then wiped the tobacco juice off his lower lip.

The second man stepped forward. He was a large-boned, sprawling fellow with a prominent waxy nose and jug ears. He wore a brown hat, a pale red neckerchief, a brown wool vest with a braided leather watch fob, a striped grey shirt, a brown belt and holster with a dark walnut-handled six-gun, scuffed brown boots, and spurs with jingle-bobs. He cocked his head back as he offered his hand and said, "George Call." As they shook hands, Call added, "We ride for the Rockin' B. Owned by Gus Aldredge. You'll meet him soon enough, I 'spect."

Fontaine glanced from Call to Barrett. "I try to get along. I hope we all do. Get along, that is."

Call leaned back as he hung his thumb on his gunbelt and nudged the inside of his thigh with his middle finger. "Oh, yeah. Ain't that right, Fred?"

Barrett held his liquid blue eyes on Fontaine again. "Sure. Everyone gets along. It's the way to be in this country." His hard face relaxed into a smile. "If you need anything, just let us know. We're over west a couple of miles."

"Thanks, fellas."

"Don't mention it," said Call.

The two men turned, and as they walked their horses away they seemed to be studying the ground as before. This time they reminded Fontaine of the story of the fallen angels who looked in vain for gold as they had seen it on the streets of Heaven before they got thrown out.

The sun was straight up, and the dead tree was casting a thin, close shadow. Fontaine was sitting in the shade of the cabin doorway, thinking about wood and water, when the buckskin raised its head and snuffled.

A rider was coming downslope from the west. He seemed to be in no great hurry, as he sat relaxed in the saddle and let his horse amble along.

Fontaine stood up and waited as the horse and rider came near. The man had the standard gear of a rifle and scabbard on one side of the saddle and a rope on the other, but he had no pistol in sight. He waved and called out an indistinct greeting, then dismounted and walked the last thirty yards. He was of average height and build, with a broad-brimmed hat and loose vest. He had brown hair and a three-day stubble.

"Good afternoon," said Fontaine.

"Thought I'd drop in." The man's light brown eyes traveled around. "Did you buy this quarter-section?"

"Yes, I did."

"From March, huh?"

"From the next owner, I think. Man named Ben Spoonhammer."

"Don't know him."

"Well, he was the one with the title. Had it free and clear, and I bought it from him."

"I've got a half-section."

"Oh."

The man held out a large hand. "My name's Walt McClatchy." He tipped his head back. "I'm over west of you. There's another one-sixty, then me."

"I met a couple of others earlier in the day. Said their names were Barrett and Call."

McClatchy nodded. "Oh, yeah. They work for Gus. Farther west and a little to the south."

"So I understood. Does he run a big outfit?"

"He tries." McClatchy kept his mouth closed as he gave a

tight smile. Then as he spoke, it became evident that he was missing three or four teeth in a row on the upper left side of his mouth. "You don't know Gus. He's got a good-sized spread, and then he buys these smaller claims when he gets a chance. I'm surprised he didn't buy your place."

"Maybe he's still waitin' for an answer from March."

"Could be." The brown eyes roved. "What are you goin' to do for water? I don't believe this place has ever had a well."

Fontaine motioned toward the south. "I hauled a couple of gallons from the creek. Long ways to go to water my horse, though. What kind of wells do they have around here?"

"Depends. Charley Drake—he's north of this, next place over—he paid a man to put a well in for him. That was after he tried himself, dug down almost twenty feet and never found a drop. Paid this other man ninety-five dollars, took a couple of months to go down eighty feet, and he can pump a few gallons at a time."

"How about yourself?"

The self-satisfied smile came back. "I got lucky. Got a man with a drillin' rig, went down eighteen feet, and got all the water I want. I could pump five gallons a minute if I wanted."

"That's good."

"Like I said, I got lucky."

"And this fellow Aldredge, I suppose he has windmills."

"Some. He's got a couple of good springs, too. There's water in those buttes if you know where to look."

"So there's no tellin' what I can expect."

"Nah. What I did, was, I found my water first, and that's where I built my shack."

Fontaine shrugged. "Well, I'll just have to see."

"Sure. In the meanwhile, if you want some water, I'm closer than the crick." He gave an open smile that showed the empty space between his teeth.

"Well, thanks. That's right friendly of you."

"Got to be good neighbors."

"I hope so."

After a couple of seconds of quiet, McClatchy said, "Seen any snakes?"

"Not yet."

"There's some here. I kill about a dozen a year."

"I'll be on the lookout."

"Get yourself a shovel."

"I'll need to get one anyway. By the way, have you got your place fenced?"

"Started. Hard to do everything at once."

"I'm sure."

"But I've got tools if you need any—diggin' bar, pliers, hammer, even a wagon. Don't be shy."

"I appreciate it." Fontaine gave a sweeping glance to the pasture around him. "I'm not real fond of fences myself, but it looks as if a fella will get grazed off if he doesn't do something about it."

"That's Gus. 'Course, I've got a few head myself, but he runs his all over. And the law is, a man don't have to fence his stock in. You've got to fence out."

"I knew that."

"If you've got any kind of a problem, and you mention it to Gus, he'll say, 'I'll send a couple of men over to help you.' That means he won't." McClatchy gave his self-assured smile. " 'Course, I've been here almost as long as he has. I was one of the first to take up land when they opened it up for claims."

"Oh. How long ago was that?"

"I been here four years."

Fontaine drew his brows together. "I think Ben Spoonhammer had this place longer than that, and the fellow before him made the claim and proved up on it."

15

"Could be." McClatchy glanced around at the buckskin and the dead tree and said, "Then there's always firewood to think about."

"That's true. That little bit of dead wood isn't going to last long. It looks as if the creek is the best place to get more, unless there's any public land back in those buttes."

"I go to the crick bottom. Get a wagonload when I can. You want to go along some time, we can do that."

"Well, that's a good offer. I'm likely to take you up on it."

"Work goes better when you've got company." The light brown eyes wavered for a second and came back. "Been to town?"

"Redwillow? Not yet. Anything I should know?"

"It's like any other. Depends on what you need."

"Just supplies. Maybe a bath at some point."

"There's that, and more. No train, of course. Just a stage. But there's a post office, and a telegraph. Like I say, depends on what you need."

"Not much."

"Then you'll find it there."

"That's what I find in most places. Not much."

"You won't be disappointed, then."

As Fontaine turned north onto the main street of Redwillow, the town came into view. The street itself was broad, with ruts and potholes and a couple of dished-out areas. Wooden sidewalks and frame buildings lined each side for a couple of blocks. On the left, the afternoon shadows were reaching into the street, but with the absence of horses and wagons, the thoroughfare looked empty.

Nothing had been built more than one story high, and not a tree appeared on the main street except at the far end, where two thin elm trees rose above a picket fence on the right side.

As Fontaine rode forward, a house set back from the fence came into view. It was yellow with white trim, including four white posts holding up the roof of a front porch. In future years, if someone continued to tend the trees, they would offer shade on an afternoon like this one.

Bringing his glance back to the middle of town, Fontaine noticed that half the buildings were unpainted. The blacksmith shop on his left was rough and weathered, as was the Pale Horse Saloon. The building that housed the post office in between the barber shop and Singer's Emporium had been painted white at some time and had since begun to peel. On his right, a white building with dark blue trim looked to be in a better state of preservation. Its sign had clear lettering that read "The Gables," and below that, "Lodging." Next on the right came the general store, with faded red lettering on weathered white, followed by unpainted buildings identified as the Inland Sea Café, Swope Coal and Drayage, and the Old Clem Saloon.

The door of the saloon was open, and the sound of voices drifted out. Fontaine glanced to the west, where the sun had not yet slipped behind the buttes. He turned the buckskin to the left, crossed the empty street, and came to a stop in front of the barber shop. To the left of the hitching rail, the Pale Horse Saloon had its door closed. So much the better.

The barber showed him to a room in back, where he sat in a flimsy tin tub and poured tepid water over himself from a tin pitcher. He had had more luxurious baths, but the end result of this one was satisfactory. When he was dressed again, he gave himself a once-over.

As always, he looked older in the mirror than he did in the mental picture he had of himself. His light brown hair was greying at the temples, but at least it hadn't begun to thin on him. Creases were showing at the corners of his eyes, but the whites were still clear and the irises held their bluish-grey color. After months of seeing Ben Spoonhammer's faded blue eyes, it did him good to see his own, even as he was reminded that he would not see thirty-five again, or thirty-six.

He picked up his hat, dusty and flat-crowned and flat-brimmed. He decided to let his hair dry a little more. Carrying the hat, he walked out through the barber shop and onto the sidewalk.

The shadows had stretched past the middle of the street, and the buckskin was no longer the only horse at the hitching rail. Fontaine decided to leave the horse in the shade as he went across the street to get something to eat.

The Inland Sea Café was stuffy inside, more than he thought it should be just from being on the sunny side of the street. He was the only customer in the café, so he took a seat where he was out of the sunlight and could see the front door.

A stout woman with a German accent took his order, then served him a bowl of beef stew and a crust of bread. As he ate his meal, the woman stood with her weight against the counter and fanned herself with a piece of pasteboard. She had her hair wrapped in a tight bun, and she wore an apron over her high-necked dress.

"Hot in here," he said.

"De offen."

"Open the door?"

"Da flies."

He ate for a couple of minutes and spoke again. "Very many people come in here?"

"Sometimes."

"That's good."

"Oh, ya. You a cowpuncher?"

"Sometimes."

"Ya. Lot of them. And a few ship-heads."

"Sheepherders?"

"Ya." She brought a rolled newspaper out of nowhere and swatted a fly on the counter.

"Does the stagecoach stop here?"

"Down the street. They got the other café there."

"Oh."

He finished his meal and paid the woman.

"You come back," she said. "Better bread next time. I ran out, had to make some more." She handed him his change.

"What's your name?"

"Jim Fontaine."

"Dat's goot. You call me Gertie."

Outside, he walked past the coal and drayage business and paused outside the Old Clem Saloon. The door was still open, and he heard voices. He went across the street for his horse, and after tying it up in front of the saloon, he went in.

The furnishings of the Old Clem Saloon were more refined than he would have expected from the name and the rough lumber exterior. A polished mahogany bar ran the length of the left side of the establishment, and the back bar consisted of a high, wide mirror flanked by pillars holding up an arch. Lamps on the pillars reflected in the mirror, as did the lamps mounted in front of smaller mirrors on the other three walls and on the support poles in the middle. Deer and elk heads hung on the varnished pine walls and gazed out with dignity. In the southeast corner, a golden eagle poised with its wings spread.

Fontaine took his place at the bar, where a stoop-shouldered man with thinning blond hair and a bushy mustache, both running to grey, served him a mug of beer. Fontaine laid a dollar on the bar. The bartender nodded, then walked back to the end of the bar where he had been talking to a portly man in a dark suit and derby hat.

The only other patrons at the moment were two men who sat in quiet conversation at a table near the back. They looked as if they might be cattlemen. As Fontaine drank his beer, a man with white sleeves and a green vest lit a lamp that hung over a poker table not far from the eagle on its perch. A couple of more men in hats and boots came in and took a table. A tall man with a beard and no hat appeared at the doorway, looked over the place, and left. A fellow with a billed cap set crooked on his head strolled in, put his fist on the bar, and ordered whiskey.

Through the open door, Fontaine could see that the sun had gone down. He ordered a second beer and told himself that two beers might be enough for the night.

Other men drifted in, one or two at a time, and the tone of conversation became a little louder. Then came the gravelly voice of the man in the dark suit and derby hat.

"You're here early."

Fontaine peered down the bar, and there was the heavyset man, smiling, as he held his arm around what could only be a saloon girl. She had brown hair, long eyelashes, brown eyes, and a high bosom. She was smiling, and her teeth were clean and even. She wagged her head, and her dark hair, which was combed up and then came down in a cascade, undulated. Fontaine wished she would detach herself from the man, but she seemed untroubled.

Fontaine turned his attention back to his beer. He couldn't be bothered by things that were none of his business.

Motion in the mirror caught his eye. A young man wearing a tall-crowned, light-colored hat and a red bandanna strode past him. Fontaine shifted position and watched as the young puncher walked up to the saloon girl and tapped her on the elbow.

The portly man frowned, but the girl turned and smiled. She slipped out from under the man's arm and stepped aside to talk to the puncher. A moment later, she took his hand and went with him to the back door.

Fontaine swallowed dry, then took a drink of beer. He had expected a confrontation, but the possibility had blown over. The man in the dark suit, heavy-eyed and jowly, was waving his arm and talking in a matter-of-fact tone to the bartender. After a few minutes he finished his drink, settled the derby on his head, and walked to the door with his stomach leading.

Time flowed on for a little while, and Fontaine was about to finish his beer and leave when an image in the mirror caught his attention. The young man in the high-crowned hat was standing on his left.

Fontaine turned and nodded.

The young man was glowing. "Howdy, partner," he said. "You new here?"

"Sure am. My name's Jim Fontaine."

"Charley Drake." He held out his hand.

Fontaine shook. "Your name sounds familiar. Do you know a fellow named Walt McClatchy?"

"You bet. He's my neighbor."

"I thought so. I just took up the place east of him but one."

"Which place, now? The one with the run-down shack on it, the one they call the March place?"

"That's it, though I got it from the man who bought it from March."

Charley held out his hand again. "Well, put it there, pal. We're neighbors." After they shook for the second time, Charley looked for the barkeep and called out, "Doby. Let's have two." He pointed downward and made a circle to include himself and Fontaine. When the drinks arrived, he raised his mug of beer and said, "Here's to it, pal."

"Good neighbors," said Fontaine as he raised his beer.

"You bet. Good neighbors, pretty girls, you name it."

★ ★ ★ ★ ★

Fontaine came to consciousness little by little. The world was grey. His head was throbbing, and his mouth was dry. He was dead tired, but his body felt all on edge. His legs were restless, and his stomach was in a knot. He spit out a dry fleck of something. As he turned onto his side, he realized he was sleeping in straw.

Small fragments came to his memory. After buying drinks back and forth with Charley Drake, he had left the saloon in much worse shape than he should have been. Charley had faded in and out. There had been voices.

"He's drunk, can't you see?"

"Get him somewhere."

"Is this your horse, mister?"

"You can't leave him on the street all night."

"You're too drunk to ride."

He had ended up in the stable with his horse. That was it. He remembered the shadowy face of the man with the lantern. "Yeah, you can stay here."

He felt worse, stranger, than he had ever felt before. He was going to heave. He needed to get outside.

On his feet, he felt as if he was watching himself walk in his own boots. There was grey light in the stable, grey something wanting to come up the back of his throat. He saw light at the top and edge of a door, and he found the wooden latch. He fought down sickness in his throat, opened the door, holding himself upright to keep from weaving.

He walked past pens with grey shapes of horses. Some looked at him and snuffled. Now he was in the alley. He could let it go here. He doubled over, just in time.

His eyes watered, and circles floated in his vision. His stomach tightened, and he heaved again.

He needed to walk a ways. Down this alley. He could find his way back, and he could sleep some more. But he needed to get some air into his lungs, get his blood flowing.

Down the alley. He had been here before. Out of the haze there loomed a shape that he recognized, the privy in back of the saloon. His head swam and his stomach knotted, and he took a deep breath. He bent over, leaning his forearms on his knees. The wave passed over. He needed a drink of water.

The sky was starting to grow pale. That was the east, where the sun came up. Sure, and this was the back of the saloon. And that looked like Charley. It sure did, with his hat on the ground next to him. Lying halfway on top of that girl, though—that wasn't anything to be doing here. Maybe they were drunk. They both had their clothes on.

Fontaine shuddered. His head felt as if it was not part of him, and a wave of sickness passed upward through the back of his mouth. But he held himself together.

Steady again for the moment, he still couldn't keep his mind on one thing. He didn't know what he should do next. He needed to get a drink of water, but he needed to pull Charley off that girl.

He didn't know where there was any water. He felt too weak to try to lift Charley, but he could try.

Charley was loose and floppy, and he muttered something that made no sense. Fontaine got a hold of Charley's hand and wrist and pulled him, pulled him, pulled him until he dragged him off the girl.

Emma. That was her name. Charley said she was his girl. Charley had been pulling on her arm, and then she was gone. That was right. But here she was now.

Fontaine bent over to see if he could wake her up. But she wasn't loose and floppy. She was tight and stiff, and her eyelids didn't move.

"Emma," he said. "Wake up." But down in the bottom of his own cloudy pool he knew she wasn't going to.

Chapter Two

Fontaine kept to himself for the next week. He hauled his water in a canvas bag, and he dragged firewood, which he broke up at home. He left the dead tree standing so he would have a hitching post. Besides, he didn't have an ax. Or a shovel. Those things and others, like the Dutch oven, the coffee pot, the twelve-foot canvas tarp, and the kerosene lantern, had stayed with Ben Spoonhammer and the wagon. Funny how a man could take such things for granted and miss them now.

One day it rained. Fontaine sat in the cabin for hours, dodging leaks and watching through the open door. As he saw how the water ran off, he noted the place where he might put up a little dam. Between the ax and the shovel, he thought he would buy a shovel first.

Those were the good thoughts. For a large part of the time he pondered the strangeness of his night in town. He had never gotten so wrecked on drinking, and even though he had lost track of things, he didn't think he had drunk more than a half-dozen mugs of beer. It took him a couple of days to work out the poison—that, and the dread of what happened to the girl.

He could make no sense of why someone would put something in his drink, but he was sure that was what happened. He could make even less sense of why someone would want to strangle the girl. It was all beyond him. He didn't think Charley Drake had done it, but he didn't know the fellow. All he had to go on was Charley's friendly nature and his ending up in the same oblivious state as Fontaine. He was probably still in jail. If he had gotten out, he would have come by.

Fontaine wondered why McClatchy hadn't dropped in. The man seemed to be a natural busybody. Not that Fontaine wanted to talk to him or anybody else. A week of solitude had been tolerable.

He decided it was time to get out of the cave, though. He needed to find out what there was to know about Charley Drake and the girl Emma. And he needed to buy a shovel.

Shadows lay on the east side of the main street as Fontaine rode into Redwillow. He tied his horse at the hitching rail in front of the general store and the Inland Sea Café. As he stepped up onto the sidewalk, he expected to see light-haired Gertie in charge of the place. Instead, he saw a dark-haired woman of average proportions. She had her back to the window as she poured coffee at one of the tables.

Fontaine went into the general store and wandered past the beans and potatoes and dried apples. The storekeeper, a tall man with receding dark hair and a clean-shaven face, shook his head at the mention of a shovel. All he had in that line was a broom. The mercantile would have shovels. Down the street on the next block, same side.

Out the front door, Fontaine turned right. He noted the waitress again as he walked on. Past the coal and drayage business and the Old Clem Saloon, silent now, he came to a saddle and harness shop and then the stable on the corner. He crossed to the next block, where he found the mercantile. He looked over the selection of single- and double-bit axes, bought a shovel, and left.

Halfway down the block on his way to his horse, he glanced across the street at the barber shop and had an idea. For the cost of a shave, he might pick up some news about Charley

Drake without having to ask.

His hunch panned out. The barber ran through a slew of topics, from the recent rain to a gunfight up on the Niobrara to the death of the saloon girl. Charley Drake was still in the jug. Why he would do something like that made no sense at all. As far as that was concerned, not everyone thought he did it. But he was in the calaboose, and he was likely to stay there until a judge came around.

When the barber was finished and Fontaine stood up to pay, the barber looked him over and said, "You've been in here before, haven't you?"

"About a week ago. I had a bath."

The barber's eyes narrowed as he gave a nod. "That's right. Well, come back again."

"I will."

With the shovel on his shoulder, Fontaine crossed the street in the direction of the café. As he reached the sidewalk, a man came out the front door of the Old Clem Saloon and pitched a bucket of water into the street. As the man was dressed in work clothes, Fontaine figured he was the swamper. He waved to the man and walked toward him. The man waited until Fontaine was within a couple of yards, and then he spoke.

"Yes, sir?"

"Good mornin'. I was wondering if you could tell me where the jail is."

The man squinted. "Such as it is. It's just a place where they hold men until they have somethin' better to do with 'em."

"I understand they've got a fella in there now."

"Oh, yeah. Damn fool."

"Well, he's someone I know, and I'd like to talk to him if I could."

"Just go up to the window, is the way most folks do it."

"Is there a deputy or—?"

27

"It's just a blockhouse, an old cabin that you'd play hell tryin' to break out of. They come and check on him once or twice a day. The rest of the time, he's just there by himself."

"So I just go up to the window and holler."

"Somethin' like that."

"And to get there?"

The man pointed with his thumb over his shoulder. "One block over. You can't miss it. Only place with bars on the window."

"Thanks for the help." Fontaine dug out a two-bit piece. "Here. Get yourself a drink if you'd like."

The man twisted up the corner of his mouth as he squinted. "Thanks," he said. "I just might."

Fontaine went on his way and had no trouble finding the blockhouse. It was a small building, about twelve feet square, made of heavy logs. It had a semicircular brass padlock on the front door and a small window high up on the south wall. Fontaine stood below the window and called out.

"Charley!"

"Who is it?"

"It's me, Jim Fontaine."

"Don't know you."

"Yes, you do. I've got a place near yours. I met you that last night in the saloon."

Movement sounded inside, and Charley's face appeared in the window. He was holding the bars with both hands, and Fontaine imagined he was standing on his bunk.

"I remember you," he said. "What's your name again?"

"Jim Fontaine."

"That's right. I'll tell you, there's a lot I don't remember at all."

"Same with me. I've never gotten that fouled up from drinking a few glasses of beer. I was woozy for a couple of days."

"So was I. I was dead drunk. Nothing made any sense. Do you remember anything at all from the last part of the night?"

"Just you and me drinking beer. We each bought a couple of rounds, and then the lights went out. Someone got me on my feet and helped me get my horse to the stable. I woke up there in the morning, and then I found you."

Charley shook his head. "It's the strangest thing that could ever happen. I have no idea how I got there. Someone must have put something in our drinks."

"That's what I figure."

Charley was quiet for a minute until he said, "I'll tell you, Jim, I would never have done anything to that girl."

"I believe you."

"I was crazy about her, but I was never anything but good to her. No one can say any different."

"Uh-huh."

"I have to admit I got a little jealous, but I never did anything out of line. All I wanted was the best for her. I wanted to get her out of that life. I know she wanted it, too."

"Sure." Silence fell, and Fontaine went on to say, "Who else could have done it? How about the fat man who was in there earlier?"

"Oh, he's just that. An old fat man with sticky hands. He liked to get his paws on her. But he went straight home to his wife. She can vouch for him for the rest of the night."

"Anyone else?"

Charley shook his head. "No one I can think of that I saw that night or that had any reason."

Fontaine looked at the ground and then back up. "What do you think you can do?"

"Just wait till the judge comes around. But I don't think they can prove anything. I really don't."

"I hope not. If I hear anything, of course, I'll let you know."

"I sure appreciate it, Jim."

"How about your place, and your animals? Anyone lookin' after things for you?"

"Walt McClatchy came in as soon as he heard about it. He's takin' care of my horse and keepin' an eye on my cows. I don't have much."

"Well, that's good of him." Fontaine paused. "I don't know what else."

"That's probably it for right now."

"Like I say, if I learn anything, I'll let you know."

"Thanks. And thanks for comin' by."

"Glad to be able to. I'll see you later."

Charley held on to the bars as he nodded. "You bet."

Fontaine carried the shovel at his side as he walked around to the main street and down the block to the hitching rail where he had left his horse. When he reached the Inland Sea Café, he glanced through the window and saw that the only customer was a man paying his bill. The dark-haired waitress stood behind the counter at the cashbox, giving a perfunctory smile and a faint nod.

As Fontaine waited on the sidewalk deciding whether to go in, the other man came out and turned his way, a shape of light color emerging from the shaded doorway. The man's hat, jacket, and pants were of a matched tone like that of oat husks, and he was clean-shaven. His head went up when he saw Fontaine, and he smiled.

"New spade. Very nice." The man's full features and his dull blond hair, which might have been brighter at an earlier age, put him a few years older than Fontaine, and his demeanor was that of a good American practicing democracy.

"Thanks," said Fontaine. He returned the smile.

The man passed. Fontaine leaned the shovel against the building and went into the café.

The waitress came out of the kitchen as the sound of the doorbell died. She had a neat appearance, with her dark hair pinned up and her apron snug. She wore a blue dress with a low collar, and she had a clear complexion set off by dark eyebrows. She placed her hands on the counter and said, "Good morning."

"Good morning to you."

"Breakfast?"

"Just coffee, if I could."

"Of course."

He took a seat at the counter. As she set a cup in front of him, he said, "I don't believe we've met."

"I'm new here."

"I wouldn't have known that. I'm new myself. I've been in here only once before."

She poured the coffee. "How do you like it?"

He noticed her grey eyes and liked them. "The café? Just great."

She gave a tentative expression, short of a smile. "I meant the town."

"Oh, it's all right, I suppose. I haven't spent much time here. I live out on my own place."

"How do you like that?"

"It's a little primitive yet. I'm just getting used to it."

She drew her brows together. "Not farming?"

"No, just grassland, and not much of it."

"Everyone's got to get a start. We're not all born with it."

"That's for sure."

His attention was drawn by a small motion she made by rubbing the thumb of one hand against the fingertips of the other. She did not have the rough hands of a woman who cooked and cleaned for a living, yet they were not delicate. They had seen some work, and like her face, they had been tanned a little by the sun. She had clean, trimmed fingernails, but she wore no jewelry. From the looks of her hands, her face, and her neat figure, he guessed her to be in her early or middle thirties.

Her voice came again, as if she wanted to keep the conversation going. "It's not easy to make a living that way, is it?"

"Off the land? No, not really. Unless, as you say, you've got something to begin with."

"Do you know the man who just left here?"

"No, but he admired the shovel I just bought."

"I gather that he's got a good bit of land."

"It wouldn't surprise me."

"His name's Aldredge."

"Oh, I've heard of him. Met a couple of his men, actually. His place is over west of mine, up against the buttes and beyond, I understand."

She held her eyes on him in a friendly way, and her hands had come together in a still pose. "And your name? I hope you don't mind my asking."

"Not at all. It's Jim Fontaine."

"Jim. That's a good, simple name."

"It's all right. You hear of others called Sundown Jim or Lonesome Jim, but those are mostly in songs."

She gave a light laugh. "They need the syllables."

"I suppose so." His eyes roved over her neat, clear features. "And your name?"

"Nora," she said. "Nora Winterborne. But here, I'm keeping you from drinking your coffee."

"Don't go away." He smiled. "I've got to give it a minute to cool, anyway." He took a sip.

"Of course."

"So where were we? Oh, yes. We were talking about you. And your pretty name. Nora."

She blushed. "Depends on how you see it. Some people think

it's negative. Neither, nor."

"I would never have thought of that."

"Actually, it's short for Leonora, but I prefer the simpler version."

"I agree." He paused. "So, tell me. Do you have relations here, or—"

"I stay at The Gables, two doors down. I'm on my own, just working for a living."

"It's what most of us do." He took another sip of coffee.

After a couple of seconds she said, "So you've been in here before."

"That's right. A little over a week ago. I met Gertie."

"Of course. She's in the kitchen right now, making bread."

"That's good." He hesitated. "Do you work evenings, then?"

"No. Not now, anyway. I work breakfast and noon dinner."

"I see. Well, I don't take many of my meals in a café, and you're probably pretty busy at those times anyway."

She gave him a nod of agreement.

"I don't know what you would think of a little visit some evening," he said.

"A visit?"

"Sure. Just to talk. You know."

"It should be all right. Like I said, I'm over there at The Gables."

He gave her a teasing look. "You won't leave town on me before I get back, will you?"

She laughed. "Oh, no. I'm here for a while at least."

"What about tomorrow, then?"

"Are you that worried?"

"No, but I didn't want to seem in a hurry and ask for this evening."

She laughed again. "Tomorrow should be acceptable."

"What's a good time? Before dark?"

"Yes, I believe so. Say seven or thereabouts. Between seven and eight."

Outside again, Fontaine tied his shovel onto the back of his saddle. He led the horse into the street and mounted up, drawing his leg close and then wide to go around the shovel handle. As he evened his reins, he saw a familiar figure ahead of him on the right. The man in the light-colored outfit was walking along with a jaunty gait, and he made a right turn into the yard behind the picket fence.

Fontaine decided to ride out of town in that direction. When he came to the first cross street, he saw that the yellow house with white trim sat on the far corner of the next block. Careful not to be seen gawking, he kept his eye on the whitewashed fence as the buckskin picked up a fast walk. The first elm tree and then the second came into view, two slender trees about five feet high with narrow leaves. They stood in the sun and seemed to be waiting for a drink. Fontaine wondered whether Aldredge had planted the trees himself or had hired someone else to do the spade work—if not someone like Barrett or Call, maybe someone like the swamper from the Old Clem Saloon.

A voice carried from the shaded porch. The man in the light-colored suit was talking to a blond woman in a pale, long-sleeved dress. The woman turned her head toward the street, and the man did the same. He waved to Fontaine, who waved back.

Fontaine sat in the front room of the lodging house, hat in hand. He felt well-scrubbed for the occasion, having soaped and rinsed himself at the creek and having shaved for the second day in a row. He didn't expect many single women came to Redwillow, and he didn't want to lose any ground by showing up right off the range.

Nora did not keep him waiting long. She came through the

curtained doorway in a smooth motion, her hands together at her waist. Her grey eyes were shining as she smiled.

He rose to meet her.

"Good evening," she said.

"The same to you." He shifted the hat brim in his hands, waiting for her to say more.

"We could sit inside," she said, "but it's rather nice out, isn't it?"

"I think so. Not very warm, and just a slight breeze."

"We could walk."

"You're not tired from standing all day?"

"I move around. And besides, I had a little time to rest."

He followed her outside, and once on the sidewalk, he put on his hat. "Which way?"

"Let's get off the main street, so we don't have to walk past the saloons. We can talk more openly if we want. Loafers in doorways, you know."

"Of course. I don't like to be on parade anyway."

They went left, then left again onto the side street. They had walked but a few yards around the corner when she said, "So tell me about yourself, Mr. Jim Fontaine."

"Well, um, I didn't expect so much all at once. But there's not that much to my story."

She laughed. "Oh, just tell the part you know the best."

He smiled in return. "You mean from having rehearsed it?"

Her expression was still playful. "Or the parts you haven't forgotten yet."

"Well, all right. The early part goes quick anyway." He gathered his thoughts for a couple of steps. "Grew up on a farm in Ohio. Worked for as long as I can remember. Came out this way when I was about twenty. I had it in me to work with horses and cattle, and I ended up working for one outfit and then another. Most of those jobs lasted the season, which was all right except I was always broke in the winter and then had to get caught up. So I got on with an outfit where I could work year-round. I was paid to brand mavericks in the winter—so much a head, and sometimes as much as five dollars each. It's decent work if most of the stuff you brand is the outfit's, but after a while, as they say, your rope gets longer. You may have heard that expression."

"Something like it."

"Anyway, I felt I was straying onto the lariat trail. You've probably heard that one, too. You do quick work, and you spend a lot of time lookin' over your shoulder. You work your way into it gradually, and then one day you realize that's where you are."

He let his eyes meet hers, and she nodded. "Go ahead," she said.

"Well, I didn't know at what point my boss might turn on me. He was a contentious sort, always getting into disputes and such—never any gunplay, but it came close, and there were a couple of fistfights with other outfits. I stood up for him. I didn't know if he would always back me, though, and I knew if it ever came down to it, he'd sell me out to save his own skin."

"With the law, you mean."

"That was the feeling I had. So when he paid us off at the end of the fall season, I rolled my blankets and said so long."

"Took him by surprise."

"Got out quick. But I didn't have much of a stake. I needed work for the winter, and I met an old codger who said he could use a partner to hunt furs. He was good at trapping, and we shot a lot of coyotes as well. Then when winter let up, we took to bone-hunting. We gathered up piles and piles of those things. Between that and the furs, we made a little money."

"That's good."

"Only thing was, my horse didn't make it through the winter, so I had to buy another one. And then I made a deal with the old man for this piece of land I've got."

"Out here."

"That's right. This old man—his name's Ben Spoonham-mer—bought this parcel a few years back and never got around to doing anything with it. I think it was an idea he had, to settle on his own little place, but it sort of passed him up."

"So now you have the idea."

Fontaine turned to her and smiled. "I think so. I wanted to go somewhere to start over and avoid trouble, and this deal came up. After living hand-to-mouth for so long, I thought I'd like to have something to hang onto."

"That's a worthy ambition."

"I guess it's an ambition. It seems to have woke up in me a little later than in some people. I don't know what I can make out of a little place like this, but it's a start, and I think I've got a right to try."

"I should think so."

He felt lighter now as he walked along. "So that's my story," he said.

"Up until last week."

His heart jumped into his throat, and he almost stopped in his tracks. "What do you mean?"

"You were with Charley Drake, weren't you?"

He felt as if he had the wind knocked out of him. "Yes, I was. But I didn't do anything. I don't think he did, either."

"Who did?"

He shook his head. "As near as I can figure, someone did in that girl and then tried to hang the blame on Charley. And they put a knockout in my drink to keep me from getting in the way."

"But why?"

"I have no idea. I didn't know that girl at all. I felt sorry for her, and I wish there was something I could do, but I know less than you do, or so it seems. From what you say, you've been in town just a few days."

"I have. And I hope you believe me."

"I do. You just seem to know a great deal."

"Gertie is a good source. And the café is the best of places for gossip, right along with the post office and the barber shop."

"I believe that. And it's an interesting case, to say the least." When Nora reserved comment, he added, "You seem to have taken an interest in it."

"Haven't you?"

"Well, yes. Like I said, I wish there was something I could do. I didn't know that girl. I just saw her once at a distance. But she was young, and she was pretty, and—well, she didn't deserve to end up like that. I'd like to see justice for her."

"Would you?"

"Yes." He felt challenged, and a feeling like anger rose within him. "It's a hateful thing to me. You know it was some man who did it."

"Of course it was."

"And you wonder why he did it that way. If someone is handy with knockout drops—"

"You said it yourself, earlier. It was to put the blame on someone else. And it also gave him the opportunity to leave her dead in the alley."

Nora's voice seemed to falter at the last, and Fontaine gave her a close look.

"I think you might be close to guessing," she said, "so I'll tell you something no one else in this town knows."

"It won't go any further than the two of us."

"Emma was my sister."

That stopped him. "My God. I wasn't that close."

She had stopped along with him. Her head was lowered, and he could see her eyelids. She seemed to have softened.

After a second's thought he said, "I meant what I said. This is absolutely between the two of us."

She nodded.

"I'm sorry," he said. Then in a lower voice, "I'm sorry for what happened to your sister. No one deserves that. And I'll do what I can to help."

She looked up, and her eyelashes were wet with tears. "I needed to confide in someone, and I felt I could trust you. I hope you understand why I have to be so secret." When he didn't answer, she said, "Whoever did this thing to Emma might want to do something to me if he knew I was her sister. I don't know, but I'd rather not take a chance."

He wanted to take her in his arms, but he held back. She had softened because of her sister, not because of him. He realized that she had been sounding him out all along, from the moment she learned his name or even before that, but he didn't mind. He was glad he passed the test. She said she trusted him, and he felt the same toward her.

"Don't worry," he said. "You can count me in. We'll see what we can dig up."

CHAPTER THREE

The song of the meadowlark carried on the fresh morning air as Fontaine carved at the earth with his shovel. He did not dig deep, just an inch or so at a time, and he tossed each shovelful so that the grass still pointed upward. He had seen enough of sodbusters' work to know that whenever the original grass was cleared, the ground became a haven for weeds. He didn't like being a part of that process, but he wanted a low earthen dam to catch the runoff, and if he didn't dig too deep, the sod roots had a chance of coming back.

The song of the lark sounded again, and Fontaine paused to enjoy the morning. His gaze wandered off to the left, where a doe antelope had been grazing. She was about a quarter of a mile away, in no hurry. She had been browsing grass most of the time, but right now she was chewing the top of a sagebrush clump. She stopped and stared, not quite in Fontaine's direction. He turned to see two riders approaching from the southwest.

Barrett and Call. They rode across the western edge of his property as before, then trotted past the front of his cabin and down the gentle slope to where he stood. They brought their horses to a stop, but rather than dismount, they sat relaxed and looked down on him.

"You like that kind of work?" said Call.

"When I choose to do it, on my own place. Wouldn't want to do it all day every day unless I had to." Fontaine looked from

Call to Barrett and wondered if they were like other punchers he had known who were too proud to be seen working with a shovel or pitchfork.

Barrett spoke up. "When do you not choose to? When you're in jail?"

"I don't know anything about that. But some places where you work, you don't get to pick your jobs." Fontaine shrugged. "Of course, you can choose whether you want to work there."

Barrett gave a short laugh. "Funny you should say that, because that's what we came to talk to you about."

"Really?" Fontaine wondered if he was being set up for another dose of sarcasm.

"Yeah. The boss is lookin' to put on a couple of more hands. Time for roundup."

"I would have thought it had started already."

Call spoke. "We get goin' the first of June here. We're still a few days off, but we've got a couple of things to do to finish gettin' ready."

"Of course."

Now Barrett took his turn. "So if you want to show up first thing in the mornin', we'll see how you do."

"I suppose I should ask what kind of job I'd be doin'."

Barrett spit tobacco juice to the side, then tipped his head. "We need to see what kind of a hand you'll make first. So you might end up either a wrangler or a rider."

It had been quite a while since Fontaine had had to do a wrangler's job, but he had just counted his money the night before, and he was going to have to buy supplies again. "All right," he said. "I can give it a try."

Barrett smiled. "Sure. And if you don't care for it—well, it's not like bein' married."

Call chimed in. "Or in jail."

"I haven't done either of those, but I've had jobs before. I have some idea of how it all works."

"That's just fine," said Barrett. "The boss'll be glad we got another hand. See you in the mornin'."

"I'll be there."

The sky was still grey when Fontaine rode into the ranch yard of the Rocking B. The place was nothing fancy, with just a long, low bunkhouse on one side, two stables on the other, and a set of corrals behind the stables. The tongue of a chuckwagon was visible in the second stable, and Fontaine imagined he might get the job of cleaning out mouse nests and greasing the hubs.

He dismounted and tied up in front of the bunkhouse, where pale light spilled out of a window. He was about to rap on the door when it opened in front of him and he met face-to-face with short-necked Fred Barrett. The liquid blue eyes brushed over him.

"Ready?"

"I didn't know whether to bring my bedroll, but I did."

"That's fine. You can leave it in the stable for the time bein'. We need to saddle up." He spoke over his shoulder. "Ready to go, George."

The lamplight went out, leaving Fontaine to imagine that Barrett and Call were the only ones at the ranch. Barrett stepped outside, and Call was not far behind with the jingle of his spurs. As the three men started across the yard, Barrett said, "Bring your horse. You can leave him here. We ride company horses, you know."

Fontaine stripped his horse while the other two men brought out their mounts for the day. "Yours is in the corral," said Barrett.

"Where shall I put my own horse?"

"In the same pen you take the sorrel out of. It's got water in the trough."

Fontaine left the buckskin tied up until he brought out the other horse. It was a big-chested sorrel about sixteen hands high with a narrow white blaze and one sock. Fontaine put the buckskin away and went to work on the horse he was to ride. He took care not to make any abrupt movements as he brushed the horse, laid on the blanket and pad, swung the saddle into place, and pulled his cinches. The horse took the bit without any trouble, and Fontaine led him out into the yard.

Barrett and Call were standing by their saddled horses. As Fontaine led his horse into the open, he wondered if they were expecting a show. He pulled the latigo one hole tighter and set his reins, then backed the horse up a step and pulled its head inward. With his left hand he grabbed a hank of mane along with the rein, and with his right hand on the saddle horn he poked his toe in the stirrup and swung aboard.

Fontaine had not yet caught the right stirrup when the sorrel started bucking. The quiet of the morning was filled with grunts and thumps and rustling leather as Fontaine was jolted halfway out of the saddle. He hung on, though, and the horse settled down. Fontaine got his right foot into the stirrup, adjusted his reins, and stepped the horse out.

Barrett and Call swung aboard and passed him on a trot, and in another minute they were all three loping across the open range. The sorrel crow-hopped, and the other two riders looked back. Fontaine paid them no special attention, and the group kept riding.

Within a few minutes, Fontaine realized they were going in the same direction he had just come from. Sure enough, before long they were riding across his own land with as much indifference as Barrett and Call had shown on the earlier occasions. Barrett veered north, and the three of them raised up dust for a half-mile as they crossed Fontaine's pasture. Then Barrett made a wide turn to the west, and they continued riding for another mile until they slowed to a walk. Fontaine estimated they had ridden across what would have been Charley Drake's spread as well as someone else's.

The three horses were breathing hard as Fontaine rode up between Barrett and Call. "Mind if I ask a question?" he said.

Barrett spit to the side, away from the group. "Have at it."

"I'm wondering what our objective is here."

"Our objective," said Barrett, in his voice that seemed always to have a tinge of sarcasm, "is to cover some country and see if there's any Rockin' B horses left out here."

"Do you not have 'em all gathered yet?"

Barrett gave him a matter-of-fact look. "If we did, we wouldn't be out here."

"Well, I'm new, and you fellas are takin' the lead, but when I've gathered horses in the past, we spread out."

Call joined in on the conversation. "You might say our other objective was to see if you could keep from fallin' off your horse."

"And your conclusion?"

Call smiled. "So far, so good."

Barrett picked up the thread from there. "As for ridin' three strong, we're just gettin' started. We need to comb this whole country to the west."

Fontaine noticed that Barrett was looking at the ground instead of the far-flung rangeland. "Whose place is this we're on?" he asked.

"I don't pay it much mind," said Barrett. "One place runs into another."

"Like I said, I'm new, but my understanding is that there's quite a few different parcels out here. We've probably already ridden over three or four different people's property."

"It don't signify much," said Call. "If a man don't want other riders or cattle on his land, he can put up a fence. That's just the way things are." He tipped his head back. " 'Course, turnabout's fair play. If you don't want other cattle on your place, you better not let yours wander on someone else's."

"I don't have any cattle of my own yet, of course, and I wasn't thinkin' only of myself. Just a little consideration—"

Barrett cut in. "Consider all you want, but as long as you're ridin' for the boss, you ought to remember how your bread is buttered." He sniffed. "Forget about things you don't have any control over. We're gonna be off on the other side of these buttes in a few days anyway." He ran his tongue along the underside of his upper lip. "Look. We'll do it this way. George can go around the end of that long butte and come down between 'em. He knows the way. You go along the base of the buttes and keep an eye on all the little side canyons. I'll stay out here in the open country. These horses all know each other, so if you see one, he'll probably fall in with you. If you need to put a rope on one, that's fine. Just be sure he's got the right brand. If you get one or more to follow you, you'll have to ride fast and keep movin'. You know that."

"All the way back to the ranch?"

"That's right. We'll meet there. Sometime after noon, I'd expect."

Fontaine watched as Call spooned the bacon rind and beans onto the three crockery plates. There was no talk about work as there usually was in a bunkhouse, and neither of the other two men seemed to care that no one had brought back a single horse.

Barrett took out his sheath knife and stuck it in the table top. It looked homemade, with a thick, narrow blade and a bone handle. Fontaine had seen other men stick a knife in the table that way at mealtime, more or less by habit, so he tried not to pay it much attention, though he felt Barrett had made the gesture for effect. He was even more convinced when Barrett took off his hat and laid it aside. The short-necked man, who was about twenty-five years old, had a receding hairline and kept his hair cut short like a jail dock. A crooked scar ran diagonally across his head.

"How many horses do you think are still out there?" Fontaine asked.

Barrett pulled his plate toward him and rested his left arm on the table as if to guard his food. Without looking up, he said, "A few."

Call rapped the metal spoon on the lip of the pot. "Eat up," he said.

Fontaine pulled his plate near as Call sat down across from Barrett and gave his plate a turn as he scooted it toward himself. Call tipped his hat back, then leaned forward and began putting away the grub. Barrett did not eat quite as fast, but he gave his food all of his attention.

Fontaine plied another question. "How many men do you expect to have on the roundup crew?"

"Regular," said Call. "About eighteen or twenty." He went on eating.

"All from this outfit?"

"Oh, no. Most of 'em are from the other outfits we put in with."

"Who furnishes the chuckwagon?"

"Big Hog Thompson."

"That sounds like a Texan name."

"It's actually Thompson Bighoff."

"Does he go along with being called Big Hog?"

"He's dead. But his son-in-law runs the outfit under his name. I don't know what he knows." Call went back to his plate.

"I thought I saw a chuckwagon in the stable here."

"Maybe you did," said Barrett.

Call rested his spoon for a second and looked up. "How are you at makin' biscuits?"

"I've made a few. Never cooked for a big group, though."

"Oh, the Big Hog's got a cook. But if they make you night wrangler, you'll be his helper."

"I see."

Barrett and Call went back to eating. All three men had started with big portions, and the bacon and beans were disappearing fast.

Call scooped up the last of his and let his spoon fall, clattering on his plate. "Well, that was pretty damn good for a bull camp," he said. He pushed his chair back from the table, sprawled his legs, and drew a sack of cigarette tobacco from his vest. His nose and ears were prominent as he lowered his head and took out a paper to build a cigarette.

"Time like this," he said, "you think about how nice it would be to have a little woman around. Not only does she set the grub on the table, but when she clears it away she comes back with a pie."

"Don't let her eat too many of them dried apples herself," said Barrett. "You know what that does."

"Sure." Call finished shaking the tobacco onto the paper, then took the string in his teeth and pulled the bag shut.

Barrett made a circular motion as he cleaned his plate with his spoon. "You don't want to get stuck on one."

Call raised his eyelids as he evened the tobacco with his finger. "Depends on which one. In a way, they're all the same, but some are better than others. You might find one you want to keep."

"*You* might." Barrett pushed his plate away and drew out a plug of tobacco. With a muscle-bound motion he pulled the knife out of the table, curved it toward him, and cut a hunk of tobacco into his mouth. When he was done, he worked his lower lip so that it came out shiny and moist. Then he shifted in his seat and put the knife away.

"You never know," said Call. He licked the edge of the paper and patted the seam. "They say there's someone for everyone. There might be some sweet thing out there waitin' for me, and I just got to go through 'em one by one until I find her."

Fontaine did not know how much of this talk was intended to impress him, but none of it was new to him, so he ate his beans and said nothing.

By the time he was finished, Call had smoked down his cigarette and Barrett had spit a couple of times into a can. Fontaine wondered if there would be any coffee, and he got something of an answer when Call dropped his booted foot to the floor and with an additional jingle got his feet beneath him and stood up.

"I suppose we should get goin'," he said.

Barrett sniffed and stood up as he put on his hat. "Be a good time to trim that sorrel. There's three of us, and he got rode this morning, so he'll have some of the starch taken out."

Fontaine followed the other two toward the corral where he had left the horse. Barrett and Call waited as he took a rope halter off of a peg, went into the pen, and caught the horse. Barrett held the gate as Fontaine led the animal into the yard. Call had two ropes ready.

Fontaine held the sorrel by the halter and the lead rope as Barrett began the work. Staying close, Barrett put a rope around the horse's girth. He passed the rope across the animal's withers, in front of the right front shoulder, between the two front legs, then out and up in back of the front left shoulder. He tied the rope off so that it would not slip and grow longer. Then he took a second rope, tied it around the sorrel's front left ankle, and passed it through the loop made by the first rope. He lifted the foot and tied off the rope, but the animal would not stand still and let the man handle his hoof.

Barrett said they were going to have to trip the horse and hold him down to be trimmed. With the first foot tied up, Barrett tied onto the left hind foot in similar fashion and lifted it, and the three men pushed the horse over and onto his side.

Barrett tied the hind foot to the front foot, and he gave Fontaine the job of pulling up on the rope that held the feet together and at the same time holding and pushing down on the animal's head. With Call helping to hold each foot in place, Barrett was able to trim the two feet that were tied. After every two or three clips with the pinchers, though, the horse thrashed, and Fontaine went up and down until he got the horse settled again.

In order to trim the other two feet, the men had to flip the horse over and move the rope to the feet that needed work. Through the second part of the process, Fontaine had to continue wrestling the horse as Barrett and Call did the trimming.

The process took more than an hour, and Fontaine got pretty well bruised on his forearms. The other two men got kicked a few times as well, but they got the horse trimmed. He had dirt and dry grass stuck to his coat on both sides, but when the ropes were off and he got up onto his four feet, he shook himself off and stood still.

Fontaine put the horse back in the corral and took a couple of minutes to brush off the dust and other particles that had clung to him.

Even though he was tired and sore, he asked, "What next?"

"That's enough for today," said Barrett, without looking straight at him. "You can come back in a couple of days."

Fontaine took a second to absorb the answer. "I thought there was more work."

"There will be. Probably more than you care for."

"Day after tomorrow, then?"

Barrett's liquid blue eyes came to rest on him. "That's right. First thing in the morning."

Fontaine was resting on his bunk and examining the bruise on his left forearm when he heard the thud of hooves on the ground outside. He swung his legs around, stood up, put on his hat, and walked to the door.

Walt McClatchy had ridden in from the direction of his own place and was looking over Fontaine's work on the border of dirt.

"Afternoon," said Fontaine.

"Hey." McClatchy turned and smiled. "Seen your horse and figured you was at home, so I stopped in."

"Glad you did. I'll get us a couple of chairs, and we can sit in the shade."

"Good idea."

The shadows were longer on the east side of the cabin than on the north, so Fontaine set the chairs there. McClatchy had slipped off the bridle and put a rope around his horse's neck, and he let the horse wander out to the end of the rope and graze on the short grass.

"I guess you been to see Charley Drake," he said.

"A few days ago. He said you were lookin' after his place."

McClatchy shrugged. "Sort of."

"I'm sorry to see him get in that kind of a mess."

"It's what happens."

"Pretty unusual, seems to me."

The dark area showed in McClatchy's mouth as he said, "Oh, as far as that goes, yeah." He leaned his head to one side, in an expression of conceding. "Feel sorry for the girl. But Charley was stuck on her, and even if they didn't put something

50

in his drink, he couldn't see straight."

"I suppose."

"I've always stayed clear of those kinds of girls. One time in Ogallala, I walked down one of those hallways by mistake, and a girl took my hat off my head and threw it in on her bed." McClatchy smiled, showing the gap as well as his teeth, and he gave a sheepish wag of the head. "Lost a good hat on that deal. Pretty girl, too."

"Ogallala," said Fontaine. "The Gomorrah of the plains."

"It was pretty wild. Probably still is." McClatchy tossed a glance toward the dirt that Fontaine had mounded up. "You been busy."

"Oh, that wasn't much. Just hopin' to catch some water if it rains any more."

"It might. Sometimes it rains buckets." McClatchy gave a look around. "What else you gonna do?"

"Probably not much for the next little while. Aldredge's men came by and asked me if I wanted to work for him on roundup."

"What's it pay?"

Fontaine thought the question was a bit blunt, but he knew McClatchy was a good source of information as well as questions. "I don't know yet, because I'm not sure what job I'll have."

"That's Gus. Keep you guessin'. But he paid a dollar and a dime last year. They've got a shotgun roundup, you know. Three or four different outfits go in together."

"That's what I understand."

"When do you start?"

"Actually, I went and worked the better part of the day today with Barrett and Call. I think they were trying me out."

"Probably were."

"They're a jolly pair."

51

McClatchy lifted his eyebrows. "You must've seen their good side."

"I was being humorous. This fellow Barrett seems to have a real chip on his shoulder."

"He likes to fight."

"That's no surprise."

"He likes to fight men that are bigger'n him and older—not old men, but men in their prime."

"They've got their talk about women, too."

"Oh, Call thinks he's a real lady-killer. Even women that are already taken, he thinks they should fall all over him. Barrett, now, I guess he had a woman that was goin' to marry him, but they say he beat her up too soon, and she got smart and took off. I never saw her. Just what I heard."

"Well, if they were the only two I was going to work with, I might think twice about it. But with a larger crew, it's easier to stay clear of some people. By the way, does Aldredge go on roundup himself?"

"I think he visits. He lives in town, you know."

"I gathered that." After a couple of seconds of silence, Fontaine said, "How is he to work for?"

"To tell you the truth, I don't know."

Fontaine recalled his impressions from earlier in the day. "For a man with that much land, you'd think he'd have more men working for him. Or does he have more on another place?"

"He's got a couple at another camp, back in the buttes. The rest he hires seasonal, like you."

"I guess he does have quite a bit of land, though, doesn't he?"

"Oh, for an individual he does. He's built up. He came here a couple of years before I did, and he got some land in the buttes. Some of it's not very good, I guess. Then he started buyin' up places on this side. You know, a lot of people come out here not knowin' much, and they find out they can't make it. So when I came here, he was already startin' to buy out some of these others. He was sort of checker-boarded, but since just about none of these places have fences, he let his cattle go where they would."

"That's the sense I got. Those two riders of his don't seem to care at all. In fact, I think they go out of their way to ride over other people's land."

"They might, those two. Gus brought them in a couple of years ago, when he started to step things up."

"Oh. How was that?"

McClatchy tugged on the rope that he had tied to his horse. "Well, at first he just waited until someone was ready to sell out, and he got it as cheap as he could. But then he started pushin' a little. Like this place between you and me. Fella was tryin' to get started there, and he said Gus's men would come by and lean on him. So he said hell with it, took the offer Gus made him, and went somewhere else. Up on the Niobrara."

"That's the next river to the north, isn't it?"

"Yeah. Used to be called the Running Water. Then the next one north is the Cheyenne River. Used to be called Good River." McClatchy narrowed his eyes and nodded. "There's a lot to know about this country."

"Uh-huh. So Aldredge pushed him out?"

"That's what it amounted to."

"Has he tried to buy your place?"

"Not yet. Seems like he wants to get this strip first. I reckon he's got a map and a plan." McClatchy smiled with his mouth closed. "But I can wait him out."

Fontaine tried to picture the strip McClatchy referred to.

The neighbor spoke again. "It's a wonder he didn't try to buy this place."

"He might have tried. Maybe he didn't know who owned it

or where the man was. But he ran his cattle over it all the same.
I can see that. Probably other brands as well."

McClatchy shrugged. "Sooner or later, there'll be fences." He
gave Fontaine a direct look. "How about you? Do you think you
can make a livin' off this parcel?"

"I don't know. I doubt it."

"Gonna get some cattle?"

"I might."

"Think you'll have a family here?"

"I haven't thought that far ahead." Fontaine decided to turn
the question back. "How about you? Got plans for a family?"

"Oh, I'm past forty. I don't know that I care for kids at this
point. But don't be surprised if I've got a woman here by this
time next year." He hiked one leg over another and clasped his
big hands around his knee. "So when do you ride out with
these other fellas?"

"I'm supposed to show up again day after tomorrow."

"Well, if you'd like, I can keep an eye on your place for you."

"There won't be much here that wasn't here before, but
you're welcome to ride by."

McClatchy gave him a knowing look. "Just a precaution. You
never know when someone might come snoopin' around,
especially with no one at Charley Drake's place."

"Appreciate it." As he spoke, Fontaine recalled where
Charley's place was. It was not far away, just north of the place
due west where the man had sold out to Aldredge. McClatchy
had referred to a strip of land. Charley's place was probably on
it, and his was, too. He wondered if there was a crooked deal
beneath it somewhere. "Think it'll rain?" he asked.

McClatchy raised his eyebrows. "It could. You never know."

CHAPTER FOUR

Water ran off the corner of the canvas bag and onto the buckskin's shoulder as Fontaine hoisted the awkward weight onto the front of his saddle and wrapped the rope around the saddle horn. A gallon and a half of water made for quite a little bit of weight, and it didn't last long. Fontaine thought it would be handy to have a burro with a ten-gallon keg lashed to each side of a packsaddle, or better yet a hooligan wagon with a couple of twenty-five-gallon barrels. An image of the unused chuckwagon passed through his mind, and he wondered if there was a multitude of odd details about the Rocking B or whether Barrett and Call just liked to make things seem that way.

Early evening shadows were starting to lengthen across the land as he headed back to his cabin. The rangeland lay quiet, and even the sagebrush had long shadows at this hour. Off in places he couldn't see from here, on the granger homesteads, people would be milking cows and hearing the cackle of chickens. Some of those hardscrabble places made for rough living, but if a man had water and the company of a woman, he could put up with quite a bit.

As he topped the last low rise on his way home, Fontaine saw an object out of place on the shadowy range. The object turned out to have two parts, a horse and a man, and they were standing on the area that Fontaine had cleared with his shovel. The horse was facing east, with its right side toward Fontaine, and its head and neck blocked out part of his view of the man. It looked as if the stranger was poking his foot at the berm of dirt.

Fontaine gigged his horse into a faster walk. The stranger seemed absorbed, and he did not look around until his horse lifted its head and turned it. Fontaine studied the man and the animal as he rode the last hundred yards.

The man had a slovenly look about him, with loose, dark clothes and a slouch hat. The horse was a common-looking, dull-colored thing with prominent hip bones and a ragged tail. The saddle had worn spots showing, and the blanket was frayed. As Fontaine got ready to dismount, a curious object caught his eye. Running lengthwise to the saddle and tied to the skirts was an iron rod about three feet long, much longer than any running iron, and the front end had a crosspiece welded on it to form a T-shaped handle. Fontaine's first guess was that it was a divining rod, but he gave it no further thought as he dismounted and faced the stranger.

"Can I help you find something?" he asked.

The man had an insolent look about him as he shook his rein and caused the horse to step back and around. Beneath the slouch hat, the man had wide, blank eyes, untrimmed hair, dark stubble, and heavy lips. His mouth hung open. He wore a loose-necked, collarless shirt, untucked, and a pair of wrinkled trousers that had ages of dirt worked into them. Heavy boots with no spurs stuck out at the bottom.

"I'd have to be lookin' for somethin' first," he said.

Fontaine tried not to let it rankle him. He said, "Since this is my place, I thought I had a right to ask."

The man waved his hand. "Oh, any squatter can say that."

Fontaine's pulse went up. "I'm not just any squatter. I've got clear title to this place."

"Good for you."

Fontaine took a deep breath to try to keep himself calm.

"And I don't appreciate some trespasser gettin' cheeky with me."

The stranger poked his tongue out of the corner of his mouth. "This is open country, podner. You ought to know the law. You can't call someone a trespasser unless you've got your place fenced or posted. If it is yours."

"I think I'm familiar with that idea, along with another part of the law. If I tell you in person, like I'm doin' now, that I don't want you on my land, you'd better heed it."

The other man pursed his lips. "I guess I'd have to know two things. First off, who it is that's tellin' me this, and second, what the boundaries are."

Fontaine took in another deliberate breath. "For your information, my name's Jim Fontaine. As for boundaries, there's an old furrow plowed all the way around the property line. It's not hard to see, if someone wants to."

"Grass grows back."

"You can see the line, especially with any distance at all."

"If I was a bird."

Fontaine was annoyed by the man's persistence, but as he gave him another looking over, he did not see any gun or knife in view. "Look, stranger," he said, "why don't you just shove along?"

"You're the newcomer, not me."

"Well, I told you my name. What's yours?"

"Toomel. Ray Toomel. No secrets about me." His heavy lips curled into a smile. "Not like some people."

"What do you mean by that?"

"I recognize your name."

"What of it?"

"Why aren't you behind bars like your pal?"

Fontaine's eyes narrowed. "I don't like your insinuation."

"I wouldn't expect you to like it, but you can hear it anywhere you go. Drifter comes to town, falls into company with a whore-hound—"

"You'd better watch your mouth."

Toomel's eyes widened. "Maybe you're one, too. Is that it?"

"Look here, fella. I'll give you ten seconds to put your foot in the stirrup and get movin' out of here."

"And if I don't?"

"You've been warned."

Toomel stood with his lips pressed together, staring at Fontaine.

The seconds ticked in Fontaine's head as he counted them off. "Time's up," he said as he let his reins go.

Toomel lifted his chin. "And so?"

Fontaine punched him square on the jaw. The horse snorted and jumped aside as the man staggered back.

"That wasn't fair," he said, rubbing his jaw.

"The hell it wasn't. I warned you. Now you either get on your horse or you'll have more of the same."

"I don't take this kind of treatment."

"Then step forward and do something about it."

Toomel put up his fists and began to circle to his right. "Come on," he said.

Fontaine moved in and hit him two more times, knocking his hat away. Toomel stumbled to his right, regained his balance, and charged. He lowered his head and shoulders and drove into Fontaine's midsection, then slipped down and grabbed onto his left leg. Fontaine pulled back, then leaned over and pummeled the man three more times on the head. As he did, he caught the smell of stale woodsmoke.

Toomel went down onto his hands and knees.

"Had enough?" said Fontaine.

"It wasn't fair. First you catch me off guard, and then you hit me when I'm down."

"Once you were down, I didn't hit you, though I had the chance. And as for the first one, like I already said, I warned you. Now I'm telling you again. Climb on your horse and get out of here."

"I'll remember this." Toomel rose into a crouch, found his hat, and put it on as he stood up straight. He gave Fontaine a look of pure resentment and said, "Mark my words. You've rode into rougher country than you think."

"I've been in rough country before, and I stick up for what's mine. If you go cool off somewhere, you might see things with a little more sense."

Toomel put his foot in the stirrup, and the dull-colored horse went to walk away. Toomel stepped down, yanked on the bit, and tried again. He swung aboard even though the horse didn't stand still, and he reined it around so he wouldn't have to look at the man who had made him eat crow.

Fontaine caught another look at the iron rod with the T-shaped handle, and then the horse took off at a trot.

As Fontaine rode into the main street of Redwillow, he saw that there were still breakfast customers in the Inland Sea Café. Since he had it in mind to visit Charley Drake while he was in town, he thought he could kill some time by going to the little guardhouse first.

Charley rose up to the window when Fontaine called to him. "Jim!" he said. "It's good to see you again. What's new?"

"Not much. Maybe a couple of things."

"Well, tell me all about it. I'm in no hurry."

"Let me see. I'll start with the most recent first. I had a run-in with a fella named Ray Toomel. Grubby sort, smells like stale woodsmoke."

"Oh, him. Where did you meet up with that one?"

"At my place. I was gone for a little while, and when I came back, there he was. Snoopin'."

"I'm not surprised. He was probably nosin' around my place as well."

"Might be. He sort of mentioned us together."

"Not in any good way, I imagine."

"Not at all. Does he have it in for you for some reason?"

Charley gave a huff. "He fancied himself as some kind of a rival."

"Really? In what way?"

"With Emma."

Fontaine frowned. He recalled the word Toomel had used, but he didn't see any reason to repeat it now.

Charley went on. "According to her, he thought he was going to steal her away."

"That's kind of hard to take seriously, isn't it? Considerin' what a slob he is." Fontaine couldn't imagine a desirable woman even touching Toomel, but he knew that for a few dollars a woman in that line of work could tolerate quite a bit.

"Oh, yeah. It was all in his own mind. But that's why he's got a grudge against me."

"Whew. Some notions."

"She and I had plans."

"Uh-huh."

"She wouldn't have led on someone like him."

"I can believe that. But he's got a lot of cheek. I told him I didn't want him comin' around my place, and he as much as told me he didn't have to pay me any mind."

"Sounds like him."

"That was before I thumped him."

"You thumped him, uh? That's good. It's what he needs."

"I don't know how much good it did, but he left. Not without muttering threats, of course."

"Oh, sure."

"What does he do for a living, anyway?"

"Not much. He picks up work here and there, mostly around freighters. Anytime someone needs a watchman, or a man to look after animals for a while. He lives in an old shack on the original stage line, before they built the town and put the station here."

"He's not a cowpuncher, is he?"

"Not that I know of. Why?"

Fontaine looked around, then lowered his voice. "Aldredge's men came by and said I could go to work for him if I wanted. Roundup starts in a few days. I was hopin' not to end up on the same crew with someone like this fellow."

"Not that I would expect."

"Good. Those other two are enough."

"Have you gotten to know them at all?"

"I went to work with the two of 'em for a day. Now that I think of it, Toomel might have known about it and thought I was still there. Does he know them?"

"He knows everybody, at least from a distance. But I don't know how thick he is with them."

"Could be just a coincidence. I didn't think of it till now. As I give it more thought, he could have been riding back from your place. Anyway, he stopped at mine to look at a little piece of work I'd done."

"What was that?"

"Nothin' special. But it would have been visible from a ways off. I moved some dirt to make a little dam, just a foot high, to catch runoff if we get any more rain."

"You never know. Thunderstorms can build up just about any day of the summer. Not every day, of course."

"I know. But if I can catch something, so much the better."

"Sure. You see those little dams here and there, and half the time they've got a tree growin' out of the bank."

"That would be all right, too." Fontaine waited a couple of seconds and then said, "So that's the rest of my news. Goin' to work for that outfit."

"Well, it's work. They're not the only outfit around, so if things don't work out as well as you'd like, you can try someone else. Of course, once roundup starts, everyone's got their crews, but there's other kinds of work."

"Oh, yeah." Fontaine glanced to either side again. "While we're on the subject, there was something else I was curious about."

"Like I said, I'm in no hurry."

Fontaine kept his voice low. "I was talking to Walt McClatchy, and he said the person in question has been pushing to buy up land, especially in the last couple of years."

"That's right. He offered to buy my place, and I'd barely had it a year. I told him no thanks. He seemed pretty bent on it, though. Same with this other fellow, name of Welch, lived over south of me. Don't know if Walt told you about him."

"I don't think he mentioned his name, but he said Aldredge's men gave him a hard time, so he sold out and went up to the Niobrara."

"That's the one."

"And this happened a couple of years ago?"

"About that."

Fontaine looked around. "McClatchy says that this auger seems to be interested, at least to begin with, in a strip of land that's got your place, Welch's, mine, and the one north of mine."

"He told me the same thing, and the auger, as you call him, did get his hands on the place north of you."

"Huh. Seems like a lot of trouble to go to when there's so much other land available."

"You know, most of these bigger operators don't like nesters and grangers. The little men cut the range up into pieces, and they pilfer beef."

"Still, it seems like a lot of effort. Can you think of anything else that's gone on that seems out of the ordinary?"

"Hmm. Now that you mention it, there was a rumor went around maybe the first year I was here. I hadn't thought to connect it."

Fontaine's interest picked up. "What was that about?"

"Well, like I said, it was just gossip. I heard it in the saloons." Charley lowered his voice. "Can you hear me?"

"Yeah. Go ahead."

"It went like this. There was a woman came to town, hung around a little while, and had a meeting with Aldredge. After that, she disappeared. Now I didn't see any of this. I just heard it. The general opinion was that she left in a huff because she tried to get some money out of him and didn't have any luck."

"Was she by herself?"

"As I heard it. She came in on the stage, but no one saw her leave that way. And no one knew of anyone giving her a ride in a buggy or a wagon."

"Not very likely that she walked."

"Especially in this case. They said she had a limp. Otherwise I guess she was not bad-lookin'. Dark hair, big in front." Charley made a motion with his hands as if he was holding up two melons.

"What was her name?"

"Never heard it."

"Did she have any other connections in town?"

"Not that I know of."

"Not Emma, for example?"

"Oh, no. Emma came here in the last year."

"And where would this woman have stayed?"

"Probably the lodging house, but I wouldn't know for sure."

"Well, it's an interesting story. Who knows if it's got any connection with anything else."

"No tellin'."

"How about your own case? Any idea when the judge might come around?"

"When he gets here."

"Well, I hope it's soon."

"So do I."

"Anything I can do for you in the meanwhile?"

"I don't think so, but thanks. Walt seems to be takin' care of things. In fact, I expect him to come around again before long."

"That's good."

"Every little visit helps pass the time."

"I imagine."

"Don't let me keep you, though. I'm sure you've got things to do."

"Maybe one or two."

"Thanks for comin' by, Jim. And I hope things go well for you on your job."

"Thanks, Charley. And good luck to you."

"Oh, yeah. I'll probably be out of here before too long at all."

"I hope so."

Fontaine walked out to the street and stood for a moment. He did not see anyone nearby who might have been watching or listening in. He set his hat back, dragged his sleeve across his forehead, and settled his hat in place. Still seeing no one, he untied his horse and climbed on.

The sun had begun to warm the main street as he rode toward the Inland Sea Café. A bit of activity was stirring, with a wagon in front of the Emporium and a couple of hipshot cow ponies in front of the Pale Horse Saloon. Fontaine rode onward, in no hurry, and was glad to see that the clientele had thinned out in the café. He dismounted, tied up, and went in.

The only customers were two men who looked like merchants.

They were sitting at a table near the door, so Fontaine took a table near the counter. He was hoping Nora would come out of the kitchen, and in a minute she did.

She had a neat, trim appearance as before, with her dark hair pinned up and her dark eyebrows setting off her clear complexion. She wore a low-collared, light-blue dress, and her snug apron showed her figure to advantage. She smiled when she saw him, then came toward him in a graceful walk.

"Coffee?"

"If I may."

He watched her as she went for the coffee pot and a cup, and his eyes returned to her as she came back.

"And how have things gone for you?" she asked as she set the cup in front of him.

"Well enough, I suppose."

She poured the coffee. "Anything new?"

"A couple of small things." His eyes met hers, and he spoke in a low tone. "Maybe we could talk awhile, later on."

"This evening?"

"That's what I was hoping. I think I've got a job starting tomorrow."

"Same time, then? After seven?"

"That sounds fine. I can go home and come back." He thought it would be just as well to save the rest of the conversation until later. She seemed to think the same way, as she took the coffee pot to the other table and returned to the kitchen after that.

When Fontaine finished and left, the other two men were still talking in a monotone. They paid him no more attention than when he came in. The doorbell tinkled, and he stepped out onto the sidewalk.

The sun was climbing in the sky and warming the day as he rode out of town. The rolling grassland spread away in all directions, and the landmarks near and far, including the buttes that loomed in the west, had become familiar to him. Specks in the distance were cattle, grazing as they roamed the open country.

Here came a horse and rider from the west. Even at first glance the pair looked familiar, and in another half-minute Fontaine recognized Walt McClatchy. The man wore his usual broad-brimmed hat and loose vest, and the brown horse moved at a fast walk and an easy gait. As the horse picked its way around sagebrush and yucca, Fontaine saw the rope tied to one side of the saddle and the rifle to the other.

When they met, McClatchy stopped his horse with a "Whoa."

"What's new?" Fontaine asked.

"Not much. Just goin' to town. Looks like you been there."

"I have. And there's no great change."

"Doubt that I'll make much of a difference either."

"I happened to drop in on Charley Drake."

"Oh, yeah. I need to pay him a visit, too. He's doin' all right, I hope."

"Seems to be." Fontaine drew his brows together. There were two things he wanted to ask McClatchy about, and one of them eluded him. McClatchy's horse shifted position, and Fontaine remembered. "Say," he said, "I had a run-in with a fellow later on after I saw you yesterday. I went to the creek to fetch some water, and when I got back to my place, there was this fella nosin' around." Fontaine drew short of saying that Toomel had been curious about the same bit of work as McClatchy had been.

"Did you get his name? What does he look like?"

"Not very spic-and-span. Says his name is Ray Toomel."

"Oh, him. He's a bother."

"Belligerent, I'd say. Seemed to think he could loiter where he pleased."

"Sounds just like him."

"What kind of business would he have out here?"

McClatchy had his hands together on the saddle horn, and he opened them. "None that I know of. Not that that would stop him."

"Well, I asked Charley about him, and he says this fella might have been out pokin' around on his place. I guess they had some kind of rivalry over that girl, or at least Toomel thought he did. That's what Charley says."

"Could be. I don't know much about him except he makes a nuisance of himself. And he doesn't use much soap and water."

"Just struck me as odd."

McClatchy turned one of his large hands palm up and gave a light shrug, but he did not seem to be in a hurry to move on.

"And here's another thing I heard from Charley." Fontaine glanced around. "He said a little over two years ago, there was a woman came to town and disappeared."

McClatchy's eyes opened. "What woman was that?"

"The way the story went, she came to town, had some kind of conversation with Aldredge, and dropped out of sight. No one saw her leave town."

"Oh, I remember that. They said she looked like a madam."

"Charley didn't mention that part. Just that she limped, had dark hair, and was big in front." Fontaine held his hands out in front of his chest.

"Sounds like what I heard."

"Do you remember hearing a name?"

McClatchy scratched behind his ear. "Sure don't."

"Too many strange things go on for a place like this, where you'd expect nothin' ever happens."

"Nothin' does, really."

"There was that girl who got killed, that Charley's in jail for."

McClatchy shrugged. "Well, that's true. But more often, things that are supposed to happen, don't."

"Like what?"

"Oh, they're gonna put in a railroad line, and then they don't. And they're gonna dig a big ditch, and that doesn't happen either. Then they were gonna dig up a dinosaur, and nothin' ever came of that. Not yet, anyway."

"A dinosaur?"

"Oh, yeah. You know they found a big bone up north of here, by Lance Creek, and a whole diggin' of 'em down south by Medicine Bow and Elk Mountain. Gus Aldredge said he had some confidential information about a spot at some bluffs about ten miles east of here. He had some bone-hunters from those other digs come up this way, but they haven't been back. He says they will be, just a matter of time, and there'll be crews to feed and all the other things they need. We'll see. Or more likely, we won't." McClatchy looked up at the sun.

"I guess I'd better be movin' along," said Fontaine. "Let you get where you're going."

"I'm in no big hurry. Like to get there for noon dinner, is all." He moved his head back and forth. "If I hear anything new I'll let you know. I'd almost forgotten about that woman you mentioned."

Fontaine felt a sinking of the spirits. "Oh, don't go out of your way. I just hadn't heard the story, and I thought it was curious."

"Well, it is. No tellin' if there's anything to it." McClatchy shook his head. "Never saw her myself, but other people sure did." The gap in his mouth showed as he smiled. "Said she was a madam with big tits and a limp."

CHAPTER FIVE

Nora did not keep him waiting for long when he asked for her at The Gables that evening. She came into the sitting room with a light tread and a soft rustle. She was wearing a grey dress similar in tone with her pearl earrings, and she had applied a touch of rouge as well as a muted shade of lipstick. The expression on her face was open as she said, "Shall we go?"

Outside on the sidewalk, she raised her eyebrows as if she were testing the weather. "It's not quite as cool as last time, but I think a walk might be agreeable all the same. How about you?"

"Sounds fine to me."

When they turned the first corner, she spoke again. "So, you have work, you say?"

"I believe so. It's with our friend Mr. Aldredge."

She gave him a humorous smile. "Was he that impressed with your shovel?"

Fontaine returned the smile. "I don't think so. He didn't hire me himself. He sent two of his men. As it happened, I was working with the shovel when they dropped by. They even had their comments about it, as cowpunchers will. But the work they had, or that their boss had, is for spring roundup."

"And that's starting now?"

"They said it would start in a few days. They had me show up for one day's work already. I think they were trying me out, to see if I could keep from falling off my horse. Then they said

69

for me to come back tomorrow morning. I don't know if we're going to the roundup then or if they have another day of maneuvers."

"Roundup work lasts for a while, doesn't it?"

"You can usually expect to be out for a month or more."

"Oh."

"Don't worry. I won't lose track of you. Or you of me."

"Anything can happen in a month."

A fragment of the conversation with McClatchy passed through Fontaine's mind. "Then again, in a town like this, maybe nothing will happen."

"Well, since we've decided to play our cards close to the chest, I suppose we have to be patient."

"I think so. And sooner or later, something will happen. There are a few different things that aren't quite right, and somewhere among them, I expect someone will drop a card."

"We can hope so." They walked on for a few steps until she spoke again. "What sorts of things have you gathered?"

"Well, to begin with, there's these two men who work for Aldredge. They seem to take pleasure in being difficult and contrary. I don't know if it has anything to do with anything else, but it's conspicuous."

Nora's head raised, and her grey eyes held him for a second. "And what are the names of these two pleasant chaps?"

"Fred Barrett and George Call."

She gave an ironic expression along with a slight smile. "I've had the pleasure of meeting them. Especially Mr. Call. His compadre, Mr. Barrett, sits and sulks, but Mr. Call lends himself to the occasion. He sprawls all over, speaks with his arm held out like a senator, and features himself quite the charmer. When it's not 'Sweet Pea' or 'Sugar,' it's 'Little Darlin'.' "

"Did they come in before yesterday?"

"Yes. Once a few days ago, and again today."

Fontaine shrugged. "Could be that they've seen, or have been told, that you and I are on speaking terms, and that might be part of their sarcastic treatment of me. On the other hand, it might be their natural style."

"Either way would make sense. But it's work, and I suppose you need to take it when it's offered."

"I could use the wages. Beyond that, there's the possibility that I might learn something of interest."

"You mean someone might drop a card."

"That's my hunch. Between these two fellas and their boss, Mr. Aldredge, something's not right."

Nora's eyes held on him again. "Has he done something other than meet you on the sidewalk and send his men to offer you a job?"

"I think so, but again it's one of those hazy things that's more of a question than anything else."

She nodded for him to go on.

"As I've gotten it from a neighbor of mine, Walt McClatchy—maybe you've met him, too."

"As a matter of fact, I have. I met him just today. He's civil enough." Nora gave a mild shrug.

"He's a ready talker as well."

"I've noticed."

"And according to him, Aldredge came to this area about six years ago. He took up some land, then went about acquiring other pieces of land around him. All pretty normal, I'd say. But then he stepped things up in the last couple of years. More or less pushed out one homesteader, bought another parcel, and made offers on a couple of others. All of these are in a kind of strip of land out where I am."

"Does there seem to be some reason why, other than to have more land to run his cattle on?"

"Not that I've become aware of. It's not an uncommon thing

to do for someone who knows of something in the works, like a canal or a railroad line, or something underneath like coal, or, more lately, oil. But none of those things fit here—it's no place for a ditch, and there's no railroad even coming to this town, much less out there. For coal or oil, they buy up bigger tracts anyway. And on top of that, according to McClatchy, Aldredge has tried to get some bone-hunters het up about a dinosaur dig, some ten miles from here."

"It sounds like a lot of fretting."

"That's the way it seems to me. Out of proportion."

"So you think that if you go to work for him, you'll make some sense of all this."

"If there's any sense to be made, I might pick up something. But I can't get too set on the idea that things are connected."

She smiled. "That's when you start making your evidence fit your theory."

"You're right. For example, inside my cabin, I found a dead centipede when I was cleaning out. I turned over a board, and there he was. About a foot long and more than a quarter-inch wide, all stretched out and dead. Dry and stiff like a piece of straw. Interesting, but not related to anything else I could imagine."

"Still, maybe some things will come together."

"Oh, there's more."

They had reached the edge of town on the east, so she paused before turning north. "What else?" she asked.

As they resumed walking, Fontaine said, "I had a run-in with a man who was snoopin' around on my place. I happened to come up on him, and I asked him what he was up to. He got saucy with me until we had a little tussle, and he left. I don't know if he's got anything to do with the rest of it. Charley says the man considered himself some kind of rival and has it in for Charley. Might have been out at his place pokin' around."

Nora's brows came together, and her eyes narrowed. "A rival?"

Fontaine held up his hand. "I'm just relaying this. Sharing what I heard. But apparently he thought he had some chance with Emma."

Nora stopped. "Really? What's his name?"

"Ray Toomel."

She shook her head.

"Everyone seems to know who he is. At least Walt and Charley do, and they say he knows everyone else. Does odd jobs, makes a nuisance of himself."

"What does he look like?"

"I think the word 'slovenly' would fit. Not much for bathing or shaving or wearing clean clothes. Has something of a blank, dull look about him, but he's got a smart mouth and seems to think of himself as being clever—what they call coyote bright."

"I'll be on the lookout for him." They walked a few steps without speaking until she said, "I'm thinking about what you said earlier, how nothing seems to happen and yet something does." She gave him a sidelong glance. "What else have you learned in your wanderings while I've been stuck in the sweatshop, shootin' biscuits?"

He laughed. "Sorry. Your choice of words caught me off guard." He raised his head and looked around. "There's another thing, and it may not be funny at all."

"Go ahead."

"This comes from Charley Drake as well, and Walt Mc-Clatchy confirmed it. A couple of years ago, a woman came to this town and disappeared. That is, no one saw her leave. While she was here, she was said to have had a conversation with Aldredge. The rumor was that she was trying to get some money out of him, and when she didn't have any luck, she left. Except that no one saw her leave. But like a lot of other things, nothing came of it."

"What was her name?"

"No one seems to know—at least Charley and Walt don't."

"And do they have a description of her?"

"Walt says he didn't see her, and he tends to mix what he has heard with what he actually knows. I think Charley saw her. Anyway, they both say she was dark-haired, big in front, and walked with a limp. Someone described her as looking like a madam, and Walt repeated that as well."

"Men have a way of saying things, don't they?"

"Some do."

"And do you think our friends Mr. Call and Mr. Barrett had anything to do with this woman's disappearance?"

"Not on the face of things. They came here a year or so afterwards."

"The same with Emma. She was here less than a year." Nora pushed her lips forward in a thoughtful expression. "The most common denominator seems to be good Mr. Aldredge, but we haven't seen any connection between him and Emma. Not yet, anyway."

"And I don't know if he has anything to do with Ray Toomel. That could come around, though, just in a matter of time."

Nora raised her eyebrows. "Various things could. Again, I can't be impatient, but it's easy for me to imagine the two of us collecting bits and pieces over a period of time and coming up with nothing better than the discovery that Mr. A. does shady land deals."

"I know. But if, as you say, we play things close to our chest at least for a while, we might do better than if we go out in the open and start asking blunt questions."

"And I don't want to do that. Until I know why someone would do that to Emma, I don't want anyone but you to know who I am."

Fontaine thought for a second. "This is a small part of it," he said, "but she must have gone by a different last name than yours."

Nora took a look around. "We had different fathers. Mine was named Winterborne, and after he died, my mother married a man named Porthouse. He left when Emma was little, but my mother had that last name until she died. They found my mother's name and address among Emma's things, and that is how they knew to send a wire there. They buried her here, as you may know."

"I didn't know that. I'm sorry."

"Well, she had to be buried somewhere, and to put it frankly, there wasn't money to have her transported. I'm sorry to sound so matter-of-fact about it, but I've had to be realistic. From the moment I learned what had happened to her, and knowing more or less what kind of life she was living, I knew it was not good. I was going to have to use the few resources I had in order to come here and keep myself unknown."

"All the same, I'm sorry. She deserved better."

"She still does. We agreed on that before." Nora's chest rose and fell as she took a deep breath. "Emma did not have an easy life. Neither of us did. But she fell in with a man who didn't do right by her, and she was living on her own with no means, and ashamed to go home. So she got into this line of work. The last time I saw her was when our mother died and she came home for that. She told me she was going to get out of this life, get a new start." Nora shook her head. "But she didn't get her second chance."

"It's too bad."

Nora wiped her eyes. "Maybe it's a lesson to the rest of us. Don't lose time and let life pass us by." She sniffed and blinked, and her eyes were still moist as she looked at Fontaine. "I'm talking about myself, of course. Not setting any lessons for you."

"To the contrary. It applies to me just as well as to anyone else. I think I touched upon it last time."

"Of course you did. I just didn't want to be taking any liberties and telling you about yourself."

"Well, that's all right. No need to apologize, though."

"Thank you."

"And if it helps you see your own way, so much the better."

"Oh, yes." Her breath came and went, almost in a sigh. "I've got to settle this thing about Emma, of course, and then see about getting my own affairs into a new order." She gave him a look that he interpreted as a kind of apology. "As you may have gathered, I don't have a great deal making claims and demands on me." She waved her hand. "Certainly no husband or anything like that." She paused, as if uncertain. "I don't want to trouble you with . . . unimportant details."

He gave a toss of the head and a light smile. "You can tell me as much as you care to." His smile broadened. "Some of it might be pertinent. After all, you got my life story out of me last time."

She laughed. "Some of it, anyway."

They came to a stop at the northern edge of town. The sun had slipped behind the buttes, but the sky overhead was still light. A hooting sound came from above.

"Is that a bird?" she asked. "That honking sound?"

He tipped his head back. "Yes, it is. Some people call them nightjars. Others call them bullbats. There are a few different kinds. They float on the air in the late afternoon and early evening and catch bugs."

"Like swallows." She put her hand to the back of her head as she looked up.

"Kind of. But they're up a ways higher, and they don't dart

around." The sound came again. "There's one."

"Oh, yes. I can see it now." She lowered her head and motioned with her hand toward the left. "Shall we go this way?"

"Might as well." They resumed walking.

"Where were we now?"

"You were going to tell me your life story." In a more straightforward tone, he said, "If you'd like, we can walk on the other side of the street. That's Aldredge's place up ahead on the left. The one with the picket fence."

"Why don't we. And I'll save my story until we cross the main street there." As they crossed the side street, she said, "It doesn't take long to walk around the whole town, does it?"

"No, it doesn't. A night watchman could make his rounds once an hour and still have plenty of time to rest."

They walked the two blocks without speaking, and neither of them turned to look at Aldredge's house or yard. When they had crossed the main street, Nora spoke again.

"I know you're supposed to keep an open mind and not judge things ahead of time, just on the basis of hearsay, but I don't have a good feeling about that man. It's almost like—what do they call it?—a presentiment. Yes, a premonition. That story about the limping woman seems all too probable."

"It would be interesting to know what business she was on."

Nora pursed her lips. "Maybe we'll find out, and maybe we won't."

A cottontail rabbit darted away from their path and disappeared under a heap of cast-off shingles.

Nora went on to say, "Anyway, about my story. I was born, as was my sister, in North Platte, Nebraska. As I told you earlier, my mother married twice. We didn't have much when Mr. Porthouse left, and for a girl in that situation, getting married is a usual way out. So when I turned eighteen, I combined my fortunes with a man who didn't have any more than I did. But he was a good talker, and we got along in a reasonable way for about six weeks until things fell in like a house of cards. He worked in dry goods, and he got caught with his fingers in the till in the store where he worked in North Platte. While they had him in safe keeping, they found out he was wanted in Dubuque, Iowa, for embezzling a pretty good sum from a haberdashery there."

She paused in her story as if to give him a chance to make a comment, but he said nothing.

"It was evident," she went on, "that I didn't have much of a future with him. The man he worked for advised me to get an annulment, which I did, but not without quite a bit of trouble on my part. Meanwhile, I went to work in a bakery, where I earned enough to pay off my debts and legal expenses. I went back to live with my mother and would have done all right if I hadn't persisted in the idea that a woman's place was in her own home with a man to provide for her. So I married again, set up a happy home with a man who worked for the railroad company as a baggage man and sometimes conductor. He came and went, and I was used to his not having a regular daily schedule. Until he was shot dead one night for trying to break into the safe of a shipping company. So that was the end of my short career as Mrs. Stanley Wheeler."

"What was the first man's name?"

"Miller. But they might as well have been Hunter and Fowler." She gave him a look of frank admission. "As you can imagine, I've wondered why I ended up with the types that I did. I think it was more than just luck." She widened her eyes and continued. "At any rate, to get out of the stigma of having Mr. Wheeler's name, I went to the trouble and expense of going back to my maiden name, and I went to live with my mother again. I worked for a few years at the work I'm doing now, and then I took a job as an office girl. I learned to use a typewriter."

"That must have been interesting."

"At times. At others, it's just long drudgery. But it's honest work, and it's better than being tied to an embezzler, a forger, or some other kind of thief."

"Was there a forger in there somewhere?"

"No, but I've known of a couple since I've been in the line of preparing and handling documents, and I was sorry for their wives."

"So, do you still do that kind of work?"

"It's what I was doing when all of this came up. I was living in my mother's house, keeping it up and paying my own expenses. And that was about it. I've thought of going somewhere else and starting over, but it's not an easy thing to do, even for people in better circumstances than Emma was." Nora gave a modest smile. "It seems as if we've each got our version of that, doesn't it?"

"Seems like it. Maybe those of us who are in those circumstances, of trying to get a new start, have a tendency to cross paths. Those who get on a definite track early on and just stay there, I guess we meet them, too, but we don't spend much time with them."

"That's true. They're busy with their lives. Work and family and church." She stopped at the edge of the prairie. "Well, here we are again. I suppose we go left." As they moved on, she said, "By the way, do you know if Mr. Aldredge has a family?"

"I saw him with a person I assume was his wife. On their front porch. I don't know if they have any children."

"He seems like the type that in a larger town would be doing civic work."

Fontaine shrugged. "Maybe he hopes to do that here, if the town ever grows. Hard to say. Now that I think of it, people like that go to places that are growing, or once they are at a place, they try to make things grow."

"From what you've said, he seems to tend to his own little empire, his personal interests. Not that civic leaders don't work on their own wealth, of course. Those enterprises can go hand in glove."

Fontaine considered what she said. "I think I agree with you on both parts." He took note of the long shadows cast by the distant buttes, and he realized his visit was probably more than half over. "Getting back to the present," he said, "there's a chance I won't see you for a while after this evening."

"I wish things were more convenient."

"I'll keep my eyes and ears open, and I'm sure you'll do the same."

"What if something happens here?" she asked.

"You mean like something—?"

"Big. I don't know what it would be, but let's say, something that would change the way we're going about this."

He nodded. "If something blows wide open."

"Yes. It's hard for me to imagine what it would be, but it could happen."

"Well," he said, "let's try this. If it's something big, and you would be the judge of that, maybe you could get a message to me. Not just a regular letter. It could take forever, and it might fall into the wrong hands. Think more of sending a message by someone dependable."

"Who would that be?"

Fontaine frowned. "I don't know. Maybe Charley Drake, if he gets out of the lock-up, or maybe Walt McClatchy, though I hesitate with him because I think he tends to blab."

"We'll see," she said. "I hope it doesn't happen, but I need to have some kind of idea in case something does blow open."

"Sure. But my sense is that things are going to move pretty slow until one of us starts pushing for information."

"Maybe we can plan to do that when you get back, if nothing

much has happened in the meanwhile."

"That's a good idea. Let's call that our plan."

She looked at him and smiled as she held out her hand. "Put 'er there, partner."

He laughed as he took her hand. "Mighty fine."

"Don't forget about me."

"I won't, and I'll see you as soon as I get back."

They made the last turn in their walk. As the lodging house came into view up ahead, Nora said, "It looks as if there's not much left to our promenade."

"It's been a good visit."

"Yes, it has been. And a nice evening as well. I'm sure the weather will get warmer when you're out on the range."

"You can expect just about anything—wet, cold, heat, wind, hail—but things ought to heat up in general."

"I'll think about you, especially when the weather looks threatening."

"I'll think about you, too, especially when the weather is mild and sunny."

"Well, you're a bit gallant, aren't you, Mr. Fontaine?"

"Can't help myself."

When they reached the steps of The Gables, he took off his hat as he held out his hand. "It's been a pleasure."

Her grey eyes had a shine as they met his. "It has been," she said. "And I wish you safe travels."

"Thanks." He winked. "I'll see you as soon as I can."

He stood watching as she went into the house. When the door closed, he turned and walked down the sidewalk to the hitching rail where he had left his horse. As he gathered the reins, he thought of the work to come. He might not be back to this town for a month or more.

He looked across the street at the Pale Horse Saloon, and he was curious to know what the place looked like inside. But a little twinge told him that from a God's-eye view, there might be something crass in leaving a woman at her door and going straight across the street to a saloon. With some sense of humor directed at himself, he led his horse down the street to the Old Clem.

CHAPTER SIX

The interior of the Old Clem Saloon glowed with lamplight and mirrors. The deer and elk heads on the varnished pine walls cast their own small shadows, as did the golden eagle in the back corner. The light above the poker table had not been lit yet. A haze of tobacco smoke hung in the air, and a low tone of mixed voices served as background for a man who stood playing a fiddle and singing a song.

> *Where the Niobrara wanders*
> *On its journey to the sea,*
> *My mind drifts back in memory*
> *To thoughts of you and me.*

> *When the silver dew of springtime*
> *Lay light upon the land,*
> *And love was free and open*
> *'Tween a woman and a man.*

The singer had his hat upside down on the table in front of him, and his voice was plaintive as he sang with his eyes closed or nearly so.

Fontaine took a place at the bar and saw himself in the high, wide mirror. The stoop-shouldered bartender with thinning hair and a bushy mustache took his order and returned with a mug of beer. As Fontaine took a drink, he looked around at the clientele.

A few men stood along the bar, and a couple of men sat at one of the tables. Fontaine did not recognize any of them. He had thought he might see the portly man in the dark suit, but he did not see anyone who bore even a faint resemblance. Then from the dusky region beyond the far end of the bar there emerged a man he did recognize. It was the swamper, carrying a pail of sawdust in one hand, dipping into it with the other, and scattering the yellowish granules on the floor.

He worked his way along the bar, behind the men who stood there, and turned from one side to the other as he spread the sawdust. When he came to Fontaine, he stopped and gave a look of recognition.

"Well, hullo, guv'nor," he said.

"Evenin'."

The man's left eye squinted. "How are you gettin' along?"

"Well enough, I suppose."

"Can't ask for more." The man leaned toward Fontaine and spoke in a low voice. "Havin' any luck?"

Fontaine shrugged.

"I understand you're lookin' to find out more about someone."

Fontaine imagined he meant the girl, Emma, but it occurred to him that the swamper might mean someone else. Fontaine frowned. "I don't know."

The swamper winked. "A word to the wise. Look up a pair of birds named Penfield and Pomeroy." Then with exaggerated motion the man leaned the other way and tossed out a handful of sawdust. As if to cover up for having spoken, he began to whistle in a painful rendition of the tune the fiddler was playing. Fontaine dug a two-bit piece out of his pocket and slipped it into the swamper's hand.

"Thanks," said the man.

"And thanks to you." Fontaine turned to the bar to finish his beer. As he saw himself in the mirror, he had an uncomfortable sense of being on public view. People knew who he was and that he was looking for information. With a little imagination, he could see Walt McClatchy in the mirror.

Fontaine turned away from the bar. The swamper had moved on, the singer still had his eyes closed or nearly so, and no one in the saloon seemed to be paying Fontaine the slightest attention. For the moment at least, it was good to feel ignored.

As he rode through the grey light of morning, Fontaine pondered the same questions that had run through his mind on the way home the night before. Who were Penfield and Pomeroy? Did they have anything to do with Emma, or had the swamper been referring to the limping woman? Or was it Charley Drake? After all, Fontaine first met the swamper when he was asking how to find the jail.

Dawn was beginning to show in the east when he knocked on the bunkhouse door. A voice that sounded like Barrett's told him to come in.

Barrett and Call, both hatless, sat at the table with coffee cups in front of them. Call was smoking a cigarette, and Barrett was cleaning his fingernails with his bone-handled knife. An overhead kerosene lamp lit the room, and the smell of fried food hung in the air with the cigarette smoke.

Barrett flipped the knife in the air, caught it with the handle flat in his palm, and put it in his sheath.

"Good mornin'," said Fontaine.

Barrett gave him a brief, cold stare. "We'll see what's good about it."

Call sat up in his chair, and the legs made a scraping sound on the floor. "Didn't know if you'd show up."

"No reason not to."

Call wrinkled his nose. "Man gets a day off, he's likely to go out and get drunk." He hiked his right boot onto his left knee and hung his hat on the toe of the boot.

Fontaine smiled. "Not till payday."

"Might be a long ways off," said Barrett as he rose from his chair. "Lots of work to do first." He ran his hand over the top of his head, where his receding hairline and the crooked scar showed, and he put on his hat.

Call squared his shoulders and took another drag on his cigarette. "I'll be right out."

Barrett led the way with Fontaine a few steps behind. Outside, the morning had grown lighter. Barrett walked toward the stable, then stopped in the middle of the yard.

"We've got to pull that wagon out and work on it."

"I thought we weren't using it." As soon as he spoke, Fontaine wished he hadn't. He had come with his mind set not to ask any questions about what they were going to do, and he had already slipped.

Barrett scowled. "Who the hell said anything about using it or not using it?"

Fontaine shrugged. "I thought we were using someone else's chuckwagon."

"Maybe we are, but that doesn't mean we don't need a bed wagon. We need to pull this son of a bitch out of there, take the box off, and grease the axles. Any other questions?"

"That first one wasn't really a question." Again, the words got out ahead of him. He bore down on himself, told himself not to let the other man rile him.

Barrett faced him and gave him the cold stare. "It was the same as one."

Fontaine didn't answer. He stood still as Barrett opened and closed his hands. The scrape of a door sounded, followed by the jingle of spurs as Call stepped out of the bunkhouse. He brought a glow to the end of his cigarette, dropped the butt, and ground it with his boot sole. He pulled his watch out by the braided leather fob, and after skimming a glance at it, he put it away.

Barrett spoke again. "You know what would be the best thing for you?"

"What?"

"Not to ask questions. Quit bein' nosy."

Fontaine gave a narrow look as he stole a glance at the chuckwagon. "I'm not sure that I follow you."

"Pshaw. You've been nosin' around ever since you came here."

"Here?" Fontaine pointed to the ground.

"Oh, don't act like a dummy. You know what I mean."

"I'm sure I don't."

Barrett took a step closer. "I'll spell it out. Redwillow and the Buttes. You come here and act like a nester, and all you do is snoop around."

"I think you've got me figured wrong."

"I'm sure I don't." Barrett waited a second to let the mockery sink in. "And we don't like it. You understand?" Barrett took a quick step forward and shoved Fontaine in the chest with both hands.

Fontaine stumbled backwards and fell on his right side. He was in no hurry to get up, as Barrett stood over him with his fists doubled. Barrett was an ugly picture of a compact, round-muscled, short-necked man glaring down at him.

"Come on, get up."

"Is this why you had me come out here, so you could shove me around?"

"We had you out here," said Barrett in his taunting tone, "because there's work to do. But while we're at it, we thought we'd tell you that askin' questions ain't good for a man's health in this country."

Fontaine almost said, "Or a woman's," but he was able to hold his tongue. Instead, he said, "Well, I came here to work, not to fight. But I don't think much of working for an outfit where I'm goin' to be bullied around." He got up onto his feet.

Barrett said, "Then it might be mutual, because we don't think much of snoops. I've known of men who have had their nose cut off for that." When he didn't get a rise out of Fontaine, he said, "You can leave anytime."

"I will." Fontaine brushed himself off and walked to his horse. He untied the reins, led the buckskin out a couple of steps, and swung aboard. "Give my regards to your boss," he said.

"Wouldn't think of doing otherwise," said Barrett.

Fontaine took him for the type who liked to get in the last word. Call, on the other hand, seemed content to stand by with his thumb on his gunbelt as he nudged the inside of his thigh with his middle finger.

Fontaine set the last rock in place and stood up. The little pyramid was no more than a foot high, but he thought it was an adequate marker. Standing on the southeast corner of his property, he swept his gaze over the hundred-and-sixty acres. The sooner he could have the other three corners marked, the better he would like it.

He wasn't going to get it all done in an instant, though. It had taken him well over an hour to find these first twelve rocks, none of them any bigger than a deer heart. He wasn't sure he would find another twelve on his own land, and he assumed he would have to fetch the last two piles from the creek.

The buckskin perked up. Fontaine followed the horse's line of vision and saw a buggy moving his way. He guessed it was coming from town.

He stayed put and waited for the vehicle to come closer. It was a buckboard style, four-wheeled, and it was covered like a brougham or a coupé. It cut a nice figure, as it had a shiny tan color and was pulled by a pair of palominos. The man driving was wearing light-colored clothes as well, and Fontaine had a good idea of who it was.

As the wagon drew closer, Fontaine saw that the driver was indeed Aldredge. A hundred yards out, the man waved, then slowed the horses so that they covered the last fifty yards at a walk.

"Good afternoon," the driver called out.

"How do you do?"

"Just fine, thanks." The man smiled. "I'm Gus Aldredge. I believe we met on the street one day, though we didn't introduce ourselves."

"That's right. I'm Jim Fontaine."

Aldredge smiled again. "I understand you worked at my ranch for a little while."

"I did."

"I'm sorry things didn't work out any better. I want you to know there are no hard feelings. Not on my side."

"I appreciate your saying so."

"I know that Fred isn't always easy to get along with. He's a dependable man for me, though, so I keep him on."

Fontaine smiled. "It's your ranch. And your choice on how to run it."

"Well, I know that, of course. But right's right, and fair's fair, and I want to make sure you get paid for the work you did."

"I worked just the one day, and it wasn't a full day at that."

"As I understand it, you showed up two days. In my mind, it's only fair you get paid for both." Aldredge's brows narrowed. "What kind of wage did Fred mention to you?"

"Actually, we didn't get that far. I had the impression that it would depend on what job I ended up doing."

"Probably would. I'll tell you, my men make anywhere from a dollar to a dollar and a quarter a day. What with the trouble you went to and all, what would you think of three dollars?"

"I'd think it was generous."

"Well, here, then." Aldredge reached into his vest pocket and held out his hand.

Fontaine stepped close and let the three silver dollars fall into his hand. "Thank you."

"And thank you for your effort." Aldredge sat back and looked out at the landscape. "So this is your acreage, is it?"

"Yes, sir."

"What do you plan to do with it?"

"I haven't got a detailed plan as of yet, but the obvious idea would be to run a few cattle on it."

Aldredge gave him a sincere look. "That's hard, isn't it? Try to make anything off a few head."

"Got to start somewhere."

"I know. And here's how my sympathy goes for you little fellas." He shook his head. "The way this land is sewed up, it'll be hard for you to get any bigger. Even if you were able to get another quarter-section, it still wouldn't be enough. You take someone like me, though, I've got over a couple thousand acres all together, so I can make it as it is. Then any little bit I can add to it helps out. You follow me on that, don't you?"

"Oh, sure."

"So in reality, this land would serve a better purpose if it were—" Aldredge paused as if to pick his words.

"Yours."

"Well, yes. I didn't want to put it so bluntly."

"That's quite all right. I follow your line of thinking, and there's nothing outlandish about it. I just don't care to sell my place."

"Of course not. You just got it, and it's a new idea. But if you look at it in another way, you could turn a few dollars before you put any more into it."

"There's logic to that as well, but, no, thanks."

Aldredge's brows tightened again as he got down to business. "I'll put it this way. I've been buying this land at a dollar an acre. Some I got for ninety cents. I don't know how much you paid, but if it was more than a dollar you got skinned. So that's what I came prepared to offer you. A dollar an acre."

Fontaine gave a light shake of the head. "Thanks all the same, Mr. Aldredge. There's nothing wrong with your offer or the way you made it, but I'm not interested. And I'm not playing hard to get. I know people are paying a dollar and a quarter for land like this in some places, but even if someone offered me that much, I wouldn't take it. Like you yourself said, this is a new enterprise for me. I'm not ready to turn right around and give it up."

"Suit yourself." Aldredge's gaze wandered out across the land and came back to Fontaine. "Maybe after a year you'd be glad to take what I offered today." He smiled. "But who knows what I'll be offering a year from now."

Fontaine returned the smile. "Who knows. But everything starts all over, doesn't it?"

"It sure does." Aldredge began to finger the reins. "At any rate, I'm glad we're square on that little bit of work you did."

"Oh, yes."

Aldredge took in a breath as if he was getting ready to go. Then he relaxed and said, "By the way, how do you get along with Walt McClatchy?"

"Just fine. He's very neighborly."

"Isn't that right? He's the best." Aldredge gathered the reins. "Well, so long. It was good to talk to you."

"You bet."

Aldredge shook the reins, and the palominos broke into a trot. Fontaine stood back and watched as the buckboard cut across the corner of his property.

★ ★ ★ ★ ★

Fontaine brushed his hands on one another as he admired his second small pyramid of rocks. Sitting on the southwest corner of his property, it would be visible to riders like Barrett and Call. Although it would not deter them from riding on his land, they would see it and know what it stood for.

He put his hands on his hips and surveyed the land around him. The shadows had begun to stretch at the end of the day. It had taken him so long to gather this second bunch of rocks that the afternoon had gotten away from him. He would have to go to the creek for the other two markers.

The land looked different at this time of day than it did in full sunlight, and it changed even more as night drew closer. Even in daylight, the landscape changed with perspective. A man moving across country, whether on foot or on horseback, learned to look in back of him to see what things looked like from the opposite direction. An old bunkhouse cook who had been a prospector and a wanderer said it was a good practice to bend over and look at the land backwards and upside down. Fontaine had tried it when no one was around, and it made him feel silly. But on a couple of occasions, certain land formations had been interesting to see that way.

Fontaine led the buckskin and ambled north along the edge of his land. After a while the land sloped upward. He was pretty sure it was one of two hills he had seen from the middle of his property as he looked west. The hills stretched down from the buttes with a broad area between them.

When he slowed at the crest of the hill and peeked over, he saw that he was right. The land looked different from this angle and in the fading light, and he felt satisfied not only in being right but in gaining this new view of it.

A dusky object caught his eye. Fontaine held still, and he was glad he hadn't climbed into full view. At first he thought the object was a large deer venturing out to feed in the evening shadows, and then he saw that it was a horse. The animal was of a dull color, not sleek and shiny. Fontaine strained his eyes for a second and relaxed. Beyond the horse he made out the shape of a man in a bent posture. The man was making a brief, back-and-forth motion. No sound carried, and the scene had a strange, silent quality. The man shifted position and began his motion again. The horse switched its tail. The man stood up. Fontaine's eyes had adjusted enough that he could make out the details.

The man was Ray Toomel, and he was poking at a barrow of earth with his iron rod.

Fontaine let out a low, quiet breath. People poked in the ground to find things that were buried—cashboxes, bags of coins, dead bodies. No wonder Toomel had been curious about the ridge of dirt on Fontaine's place.

He was on someone else's property now—Aldredge's, as Fontaine had understood. He wondered if Aldredge knew, and he figured it was not his business to tell him. Toomel's work had a secretive air about it. If Aldredge didn't know, that was his problem. If he did know, and Fontaine mentioned it, it could become a problem for Fontaine. Whatever the case, Toomel was not on Fontaine's property, so Fontaine had no stake in it. Furthermore, he would much rather not have Toomel know he had seen him, so he backed away a few steps until the crest of the hill closed off his view. Then he led his horse downhill, taking it slow, until he was on level ground again. After a backward glance that showed nothing, he put his foot in the stirrup, swung aboard, and rode back to his cabin in the gathering dusk.

CHAPTER SEVEN

The buckskin was standing on its own shadow when Fontaine finished putting the fourth pile of rocks in place. Now that he was done with the job, he thought it might have been interesting to scour the country for animal skulls to mark the boundaries, as he had known of men doing where three or four big property lines came together. But he had had enough of bone-picking. It took a huge pile to make any weight at all, and the few skulls and bones he had seen since he had come to the Dunstan Buttes had seemed to him mere picayunes.

Back at his cabin he ate his remaining piece of flat bread and washed it down with a can of tomatoes. On his last trip to the creek he had brought back a bag of water. He took a sip from it now and left it hanging on the wall. He could get a full drink of water, plus wash his hands and face, in town.

Fontaine chose not to drink at the public well. Instead he skirted town on the north edge and headed for the creek. As the buckskin drank, Fontaine moved a couple of yards upstream and washed his hands and face. When he felt refreshed on the outside, he cupped his hands and drank from the cool water.

Drops fell from his face as he stood up and settled his hat on his head. Off to the north, the rangeland was pale green and peaceful, interrupted only by dark spots representing trees along the course of Ossian Creek. The stream flowed east out of the far end of the Dunstan Buttes, ran south for a couple of miles, and made an oxbow here before it flowed again to the east. At the wide spot on the turn, just downstream from where the buckskin dipped its muzzle, the creek fed a patch of red willows that gave the town its name.

Fontaine crouched again, tipped back his hat, and lowered his face to the clear water with the pebbly bottom. He splashed himself as before and sat back on his heels, enjoying the moment of being off by himself and detached from everything. He didn't have any reason not to want to be seen on the main street, but he was in no hurry to go there. He could listen to the gurgle of the creek for a couple of more minutes, and then he could pay his first visit of the day.

The window of the blockhouse was on the south side, so Fontaine did not have the benefit of shade as he stood and talked to Charley Drake.

"I think McClatchy has a tendency to talk too much in too many places," Fontaine said.

"Oh, yeah. A good rule with him is not to say anything you don't want everyone else to know."

"I asked him about that woman you told me about, the one who disappeared, and he said he'd find out what he could. I asked him not to go out of his way, but the next thing I know, the swamper in the Old Clem is passing me a tip, and Barrett and Call want to shove me around for askin' too many questions."

"Doesn't surprise me with them. What about the swamper, though—or should I ask?"

"By all means. It was something I wanted to ask you about. I don't dare mention it to McClatchy, and I'd appreciate it if you didn't repeat it."

"Go ahead."

Fontaine glanced to either side. "The swamper said I should

find out about a pair of birds called Penfield and Pomeroy."

"Oh, yeah. Those two."

"Who are they?"

"They're a couple of birds, all right. One long and skinny like a snipe, and the other one fat like a Christmas goose. They traveled through this way—I think they were from down by Cheyenne—about the time that woman went missing. No one tied them to anything, and they didn't stay around very long. If anyone had ever found a body or reported anything suspicious, I think those two would have been questioned. But like I said, they weren't here long, and nothing ever came of it."

"Strange doin's." Fontaine looked around again. "By the way, do you think Toomel has anything to do with Aldredge?"

"Not that I know of. But he may do a lot of work that doesn't see the light of day. If you needed a man to put a dead cat under someone's house in the middle of the night, he'd be the one to do it." After a pause, Charley said, "What about Aldredge?"

"Nothing but the best. I think I told you I worked for him for a day. When I went back, his man Barrett wanted to shove me around, so I left. Aldredge paid me for both days, plus some."

"That's not all bad."

"And he offered to buy my place."

"Were you surprised at that?"

"Not really, after what you and Walt told me. I turned him down, of course."

"How did he take it?"

"Oh, you know him. All in a day's business. How about yourself? Any idea of when something might happen?"

Charley shook his head. "Still waitin'. Gets tiresome, you know."

"I wish there was something I could do."

"Go have a cool beer for me. And don't drink the town dry,

'cause when I get out I'm goin' to have one or two myself."

"I'll follow your suggestion and heed your advice, Charley."

"Good enough, Jim. I'll see you later."

"So long."

Back on the main street, Fontaine saw a man he thought he knew. The man was walking on the sidewalk in the shade of Singer's Emporium, and he was carrying a valise. As Fontaine rode closer, he confirmed what he thought. It was the swamper from the Old Clem Saloon. Fontaine waved.

The man ignored him.

"Afternoon," said Fontaine, in a voice not too loud.

"Don't know you, sir."

Fontaine rode onward. He stopped the buckskin in front of the Pale Horse Saloon and dismounted. As he moved to the hitching rail, he glanced down the street and saw the man with the valise crossing to the next block north. He was headed toward the stagecoach station. Fontaine tied his horse, stepped up onto the sidewalk, and went into the saloon.

In the dim light, he made out a pinewood bar with small panels of mirror in back. Two men stood at the far end, talking in a low tone. The bartender, a heavyset, dark-haired man with a prominent forehead and a beak nose, came his way with a rolling gait.

"Yes, sir."

"Glass of beer."

When the barkeep set the drink down he asked, "New in town?"

"Haven't been here long."

The bartender nodded.

Fontaine reached into his pocket. "What time does the stage come through?"

"In about twenty minutes. Maybe less. Do you plan to catch it?"

"No, just curious. Which way does it go at this time of day?"

"Deadwood. The Black Hills." The bartender gave him a curious look.

Fontaine laid a ten-cent piece on the bar. "Don't mind me. I'm just having a drink for a couple of friends who can't be here with me."

The late afternoon sun was glinting off the windows across the street when Fontaine stepped out of the Pale Horse Saloon. He had drunk only one beer, but he thought he should have some food in his stomach, so he left his horse at the rail and walked north along the shady side of the street.

The café at the stagecoach station was a dim, hole-in-the-wall place with four cramped tables and no customers. When Fontaine pushed the door open, a man sat up straight from sitting on a stool and leaning against the back wall. He slid off and came forward, waving his hand at the tables.

"Anywhere," he said.

Fontaine went to the farthest table on the left and sat where he could see the window and the door. He looked up at the waiter, who was pale, thin, and balding and had a disorder that caused his eyes to flicker back and forth. He couldn't have been a day over twenty-five, and he looked like a wreck.

"Something to eat?"

"What have you got?"

"Ready? Well, there's some beef stew." The man's voice had a faint slur or lisp.

"I'll have that, and some kind of bread."

"Biscuits." The eyes flickered again.

"That sounds fine."

The young man brought the order, then sat on the stool with his head tipped back as Fontaine made short work of his meal. The stew was warm but not hot. No sounds came from the kitchen, and no one walked past the window or opened the door.

As Fontaine paid his bill, he said, "End of the day?"

"Gettin' close."

"Have you been in town long?"

"Just a week. I'm tryin' to make enough to get back to my wife." The eyes flickered. "This town is dead."

Fontaine gave him back a dime from the change. "Here's this. Good luck."

"Thanks, pal. Good luck to you."

Evening was setting in. For no definite reason, Fontaine decided to take the alley that ran in back of the Old Clem Saloon. He crossed the street at the first corner, went past the stable, and turned into the alley. Dust rose from the pens in back of the stable, and dull sounds carried on the air as horses moved around on the hard ground and ate from the feed bunks. After the stable, the saddle and harness shop was quiet, as was the saloon and then the coal and drayage company. When he came to the back of the Inland Sea Café, he was taken by surprise by the sight of a woman sitting upright in a straight-backed chair. It was stout Gertie, with her light-colored hair wrapped in a bun and her white apron covering the front of her dress. Her face was calm, and she held a glass of beer on her right knee. She raised her free hand in a wave, but she did not show any special recognition.

Fontaine walked onward, behind the general store and the lodging house, both quiet as well. Now he was in a quandary. He had imagined Nora was off work by now, but with Gertie sitting out back, she might be working the evening meal. He could go around front and peek in the window, but if no one was in view and he went in, he took a chance of having Gertie come out of the kitchen. If he went into the lodging house first, he might be told that Nora was at work. There was no harm in either of those possibilities, except that he didn't want to make himself any more noticeable than necessary.

Still uncertain, he rounded the corner in front, walked past The Gables, and decided to look in the window of the Inland Sea Café. His pulse jumped as recognition registered. Nora was arranging something behind the counter, and she had her back to the door.

The doorbell sounded as he went in. She turned in routine motion, then flinched and showed an expression of surprise.

"Back already?" she asked.

"It didn't last long."

"I suppose not. The gallant Mr. Call was in here yesterday evening, and he said the 'outfit was pullin' out' this morning. He didn't mention you, of course, so I didn't expect to see you for a while. When Gertie asked me to work a little later today, I thought I might as well."

"I decided to come around the back way, and I saw her there."

"She works hard."

"I believe that." After a second he added, "I thought you might have seen me earlier. I was across the street."

She made a light frown as she shook her head. "The sun gets pretty bright." She had her hands together, and she separated them. "Here. Why don't you sit down?"

"I just had something to eat. I didn't think you would be here, so I wandered down the street to the stagecoach café." He took a seat at the counter.

"How was that?"

"I've had worse. Even when I cooked it myself."

She laughed. Her surprise and nervousness seemed to be wearing off. "Well, you don't have to order anything."

"Actually, I could do with a cup of coffee."

"I'll get it."

He watched as she went to the kitchen and came back.

As she poured the coffee, she said, "I don't suppose you've had time to find out anything new."

He raised his eyes and met hers. "On the contrary. After I saw you last, I thought I'd drop in at a place down the street."

"The Old Clem?"

"Yes." He felt conscious of having avoided mentioning it by name, and he appreciated her clearing the air. It was the place where her sister had worked, but as Nora had said before, she had to be realistic about it. "While I was in there," he went on, "the swamper passed a remark, real brief-like, that I ought to find out about 'a couple of birds.' By the way, there's not anyone else in the kitchen, is there?"

"No."

"Well, I'll try to make this quick, before anyone comes in either way." He glanced at the door. "He gave me the names of Penfield and Pomeroy."

"Did he know you were looking for information? He must have."

"That's just it. I think McClatchy did some asking for me, and dropped my name along with it. Not only did the swamper come up to me, but Mr. Call's partner, Mr. Barrett, tried to pick a fight with me about it. That's why I didn't last long there."

She gave a look of disgust. "He's a pugnacious sort."

"Oh, I think he could do some damage. I didn't give him the chance. He knocked me down, and I had the good judgment, I think, to leave it at that. So I quit."

"It's just as well. Why work at a place where you've always got something like that pending?"

"That's what I thought. So I went home to mind my own business. Aldredge came by later on and paid me, more than fairly, I'll add, and while he was at it he offered to buy my place. I declined."

His eyes met hers for an instant.

"That's good," she said. "You didn't buy it just to sell it, did you?"

"No, and that's what I told him. I don't think it surprised him. He's been turned down by McClatchy and Charley Drake as well."

"Good."

"Then another thing happened a little later. I was out on the edge of my land, along about this time yesterday, and I saw this fellow I told you about before. Ray Toomel. He's the one who snoops around. And that's what he was doing on the parcel west of me. He was actually poking an iron rod into the ground."

"What for?"

"I'd guess he was trying to find something that was buried. I noticed the rod tied onto his saddle skirt the first time I saw him, but I didn't figure it out right away. Then when I saw him yesterday, it made sense. At least a little."

"Did you talk to him?"

"No. He was on someone else's property—Aldredge's, in fact. So I just sank back out of sight."

Nora's face was clouded in thought. "He must have been looking for something, all right."

"I don't like to jump to conclusions, but your first thought would be a body."

She moved her head up and down.

"What I wonder is whether Aldredge knew he was out there. That is, whether he was working for Aldredge or hoping to get something on him."

"That's a good question."

"And no clear answer, so far at least. I asked Charley Drake what he thought, and he said he didn't know." Fontaine took a sip of coffee and glanced around. "He did have some information on Penfield and Pomeroy, though."

"Oh." Her answer was quick.

"They were in town when that other woman disappeared."

"The one who limped."

"Yes. And they left right afterwards. Suspicious, but no one followed up on any of it."

She narrowed her eyes and shook her head. "I just hate it, the way people let things go by."

"There's no justice to it, that's for sure."

She gave a short, impatient sigh. "So what do you think of all of it?"

He raised his eyebrows and tipped his head. "I think some of it is connected, but I don't know how much. A simple explanation is that the woman came to town, tried to blackmail Aldredge, and got silenced. Aldredge is still trying to keep a lid on it, and Toomel is trying to find the body. But even at that, you still have a couple of questions. What did the woman have on Aldredge, and why is Toomel out poking in the ground?"

"And, of course, the other big question. Does any of this have anything to do with what happened to Emma?"

"Oh, yes. Sorry I didn't mention that." He held up his hand with his palm toward his face. "It's so big and up close, you almost lose sight of it."

"I don't." Her face relaxed. "I'm sorry. I don't mean for you to feel criticized. You've taken on this whole problem, and at a time when you've got other things to tend to."

"Like what?"

"Like you yourself told me. Trying to get your life in order."

"Well, for the time being at least, it's all part of the same thing. Even on a practical level, if all I was trying to do was get a few cows together, I would have to deal with most of this. As for the rest, you and I are in on it together, and that's not entirely separate from whatever else I think I want to do."

Her eyes played over him. "I think I follow you."

"I didn't mean to be jumpin' the gun."

She laughed. "Jumping the gun is a great deal more direct, and I assure you I've heard it."

"I imagine so. I know how some men talk, and I've heard some of their stories about how they've presented their case."

"I'm sure." She glanced toward the kitchen. "Someone might be coming back pretty soon. While we've got the chance, could you tell me what you think we can do next?"

"I have an idea. We'll see what you think of it. These fellows Penfield and Pomeroy are said to be from somewhere down by Cheyenne. I could go down there and ask around. I think the old man I bought my place from is there now, and I can look him up as well."

Her grey eyes held him. "That sounds like a good idea, but it seems like a great deal of effort to go to. I wouldn't want you to think I'm pushing you into it."

He smiled and said in a teasing tone, "You're not pushing, and I might not mind if you did." His tone became more serious. "But Barrett did push me, and though I let him get away with it at the moment, I didn't like it, and I'm not going to let him or his boss shove me around all they want. They've got a weak spot they want to protect, for whatever reason, so I think that's a place to try to get at them. It may or may not lead us back to where we started, but it's what we have to go on for right now."

"All the way to Cheyenne? How do you think you'll go?"

"It's a full three days each way on horseback, or almost that long on the stage. I'd rather not have anyone know of my coming and going, so I think I'll take my horse."

"Oh, my. You'll have to be careful. Anything could happen."

"Anything could happen here. I didn't tell you this part earlier, but the swamper who dropped those names left town on the northbound stage. And I don't think it was because he wanted to. He wouldn't even look at me."

Nora turned her head to the sound of the back door closing. "Those two men must be worth looking into, then."

"I think it's a good hunch. Have you got their names all right?"

She nodded, and holding her palms upward, she said, "Pen," and "Pom."

CHAPTER EIGHT

The streets of Cheyenne were lined with wagons and horses. Here and there a man, most often a young man with a billed cap, rode a bicycle. Steam engines stamped and hissed; the pounding of hammers was interspersed with the voices of men. To Fontaine, after a winter of trapping and bone-hunting and a spring of riding across the rangeland, the place seemed like a big city.

Six blocks west and three blocks north of the train depot, near a rivulet called Crow Creek, he found the Good River Café. Inside, old Ben Spoonhammer sat on a stool behind the cash register. His neck was wrinkled and his shoulders sagged, but he had gotten a haircut and a clean pair of suspenders, and he was clean-shaven.

"Well, hello, there, pardner," he called out. "What brings you to the city on the plains?"

"I come to see the critter."

The old man's eyebrows went up. "Girls? You can find 'em here."

"Nah, just kidding. I think the first thing I'd better have is something to eat. I've traveled light and haven't had much in the way of vittles."

"I see you came in on a horse. You ride all the way down from the Dunstan Buttes country?"

"Sure did."

"Get hailed on?"

Fontaine shook his head. "Just a strong wind and some drops of rain in my face."

"It hailed here yesterday. Size of marbles, bouncin' up off the street. I don't miss bein' out in it."

Fontaine looked around at the modest four walls. "Suits you all right, does it?"

"Oh, yeah. Got me an old geezer from the north woods to do the cookin', and a kid that comes in and helps with the dishes."

"Does he ride a bicycle?"

"Not yet. I don't pay him enough." The old man broke into a laugh and ended with a cough. "But back to business. What'll you have to eat?"

"What have you got on hand?"

"I think there's meat and gravy. Let me ask Old Ned." Ben slid off his stool and went to the window opening that led to the kitchen. "Hey, Ned, what's to eat?"

A white-haired man whose face barely cleared the window spoke a few words in a mumble.

"Then we'll have that," said Ben. He walked with a slow tread back to his stool and pushed himself up onto it.

Fontaine recalled the season of bone-hunting. The old man had done his share of work, but he spent most of his spare time lying on his bedroll with his hands folded on his chest. "You like this better than pickin' up bones, then, huh?"

"Oh, yeah. That wasn't bad work, but it got kind of lonely and tiresome. I would do it again if I had to, I suppose. I had to push myself to put in a full day. But these days are long, too."

"Order," came a voice at the window.

"That was fast." Ben slid off his stool again, and with a quicker pace than before, he moved to the window. As he turned with the plate in his hand, he said, "Take a seat at a table. I'll join you."

Fontaine's spirits picked up. The plate had a heap of fried

potatoes on one half and an equal amount of beef and thick gravy on the other. He sat at the nearest table and took off his hat as Ben set the plate in front of him.

The old man sat down across from him. "So tell me how things are in your new country."

Fontaine speared a piece of meat with his fork. "All right, I guess. Not wet, not dry. No grasshoppers to speak of yet. From what I understand, all the sheep are farther north."

"Was that little cabin still standing?"

"Yes, it was. Not in bad shape, either. I've been staying in it."

"And what are your neighbors like?"

"Oh, a couple of 'em are all right. Nesters like myself. Then there's a fella with a larger spread. He acts friendly but would just as soon have it all."

"There's always one of those."

"His name's Aldredge. Don't know if you ever crossed paths with him."

Ben shook his head. "Never heard of him."

"And the town itself, well, it's still a few blocks long and a few blocks wide."

"It never seemed like it was goin' to do much anyway."

"A couple of strange things have happened, though. A saloon girl was found dead in the alley, and another woman disappeared a couple of years earlier."

The old man gave a painful look. "Those things are no good wherever they happen. There's been one or two in this town, but not since I came back."

Fontaine took his first bite of food. He chewed the meat, swallowed it, and went for two slices of potato. Ben seemed in no hurry. Fontaine stuck his fork into another chunk of meat and said, "Have you ever heard of a couple of men named Penfield and Pomeroy?"

Ben laughed. "I thought you were going to say Pembroke.

That's Ned's last name. Says he's related to the Earl of Pembroke. Just waitin' for his inheritance. Tall tales from the big woods, of course."

"The names are—"

"I heard you. Penfield and Pomeroy." Ben ran his hand through his sparse grey hair. "Now that I think of it, I believe I've heard those names since I've been in here. Seems like they might be the two that got killed in a roadhouse. I think so. It was up by Horse Creek. You know where that is."

"Sure. Up toward Iron Mountain."

"That's right. The way the story went, one man got 'em both. Man by the name of Wilson." Ben watched as Fontaine took another mouthful. "I hope you didn't need to talk to those two very bad. Of course, maybe it's better if it's none of my business."

"Oh, it's no bother. I don't mind you asking, though I'd just as soon it didn't get repeated."

"You know me."

"Of course. Anyway, I suppose it's beside the point if I did want to talk to them. Too late now. They were up in Redwillow at about the time that woman disappeared, so if there's anything to be learned about 'em, I'd be interested."

"Well, for that kind of information, there's a joint called the Ringtail Saloon. It's a regular gatherin' place for teamsters, freighters, drovers, and occasional rough customers."

"Maybe I'll pay a visit there after I finish eating."

"By all means. Go ahead and eat. I'll shut up. I've hardly let you eat at all."

"You don't have to be quiet. Go ahead and tell me a story." Fontaine went back to his meal.

"A story. Let's see. Here's one I heard a little while back. There's a fella hangs around a poolroom. Plays all day long, been doin' it for years. One day a funeral goes by in the street outside, and he stops in the middle of a game. He lays his stick on the table, goes to the door, takes off his hat, and stands there until it all passes by. When he goes back to the table, one of his pals says, 'Why, Bill, what's got into you? That's the first time I've ever seen you care about anything but your pool game.' Bill says, 'Well, after thirty years, I guess she deserved that much.' "

Fontaine looked up with a smile. "That's a good, heartless story."

"Oh, yeah. Easy for an old bachelor like me to tell. No malice intended."

"Did you hear that story in here?"

"Yep. From a preacher. I guess he's buried a lot of 'em."

Fontaine stood at the bar in the Ringtail Saloon and waited for his beer. On the wall in back of the bar, to the right of the mirror, a dusty raccoon was perched on a wooden shelf. Its glass eyes were dull, and its rubber nose had begun to separate from the fur.

"Here you go." The bartender set a foaming mug of beer in front of him.

"Thanks." Fontaine laid a two-bit piece on the bar. "Nice place," he said. "First time I've been in here."

The bartender closed his eyes and nodded. He was of medium height with thinning dark hair and one side of his head flatter than the other.

"What's your name?" Fontaine asked.

"Andy."

"Mine's Jim."

The man nodded again, this time with his eyes open.

"Do you know most of the regulars in here?"

"Some. I haven't been here very long."

"Maybe you can help me. I'm interested in learning a little bit about—"

"You'd be better off talking to Mike. He knows everyone." The bartender called to his left. "Hey, Mike."

A large, burly man with his back to Fontaine looked over his shoulder.

"This fellow wants to ask you something."

The man turned and faced Fontaine. He was tall and broad with a large head, long hair, and a full beard. His wide-brimmed hat made him look even bigger. His voice was loud and gravelly as he asked, "What is it?"

Fontaine decided not to ask directly about the two birds. Instead he said, "I'm trying to find a man named Wilson, but I'm afraid I don't know his first name."

"It's a common name, along with Johnson, Jones, and Smith."

"I know. I think the one I was told about had a run-in with a couple of men a while back, up at Horse Creek."

"Oh, you mean Penfield and Pomeroy."

The man's voice was still loud, and Fontaine was glad not to be the one to say the names.

"Sounds like the ones I heard of."

"Then the man you're lookin' for is called Harold Wilson."

Fontaine flinched at the announcement that he was looking for a man who had killed two others. "I see. Does he come in here?"

"Usually not. You can find him of an evening in the Aces Up. He plays cards there."

"Thanks. That's good to know."

"You bet." The big man gave Fontaine a looking-over. "Are you some kind of a—"

"Oh, no. This is just a personal interest, and it doesn't have anything to do with him, really. Just something he might know."

The man gave a toss of the shoulder. "Even at that, I wouldn't walk up behind him."

"I wouldn't. It's not a good thing to do when someone's

playing cards.”

"I mean even when he's not playing cards.”

“Oh, well, that, too.” Fontaine raised his mug. “Thanks.”

“You bet.”

Fontaine went back to the Good River Café, where Ben Spoonhammer was making conversation with a customer who was taking his evening meal. After being introduced, the man, whose name was Nolan, invited Fontaine to sit at his table.

“Ned's got pork chops and rice,” said Ben. “I'll have him serve you some.” He pushed back his chair and stood up.

“I just ate a couple of hours ago. Maybe three.”

“We're gettin' you caught up. And you'll have a long trip back.”

Fontaine took a seat.

Mr. Nolan was an older man with thin grey hair that lifted on top and was combed behind his ears on the sides. He wore spectacles and had a thin, purple nose that turned down in a point. His blue eyes were watery, and his facial skin was sagging and pale. He had a small chin and small teeth, but he had a pleasant smile. “Have you been traveling?” he asked.

“Yes, I have. From the country up by the Dunstan Buttes, south of the Niobrara.”

“Oh, yes. I know that country. *L'Eau Qui Court.*”

“What's that?”

“The Running Water. It's what the trappers called it in French.”

“I see. Did you work there?” Fontaine noted the man's flimsy grey summer jacket and narrow tie.

“I was with the U.S. Geological Survey for several years. I work at the U.S. Land Office here in town now, but at that time, we went all over.”

“Geological? Did you know of any dinosaurs being found?”

"Oh, I should say so. There were always paleontologists along, of course. They began finding dinosaurs in Wyoming in the late seventies."

"What do you think of the prospects of someone finding a dinosaur up where I am, say ten miles east?"

Mr. Nolan gave a thoughtful expression as he gazed upward. "Let's see. That would be around Chalk Butte, wouldn't it?"

Fontaine was impressed. "Yes, I think that's right where it would be."

The man smiled as he shook his head. "No, I don't think there's much of a chance there. It's not the right kind of formation. Buffalo bones, maybe. Sometimes you'll see them sticking out of a bank or a gully."

Ben set a plate in front of Fontaine. "Oh, we've seen plenty of them, haven't we, Jim? All over the plains up there by Chugwater."

"If it's what you're interested in, it's what you see. I worked with men who saw nothing but rocks."

"We were pickin' up bones to sell 'em," said Ben. "By the train-car load."

Mr. Nolan brushed at the lapel of his grey jacket. "It's a world of bones. Even Shakespeare wrote about them in his epitaph."

Fontaine took a place at the bar in the Aces Up. From appearances, its name was the most elegant feature of the establishment. On a side street more than ten blocks from the center of town, it had neither electric light nor gas. Kerosene lamps hung from the low ceiling and sat on either side of the narrow mirror behind the bar. A man with a low hairline and wide nostrils ran a rag along the bar top until he came to a stop in front of Fontaine.

"What'll it be?"

"I'd like a glass of beer."

"Got no beer. Just spirits."

"A glass of your bar whiskey, then."

The drink came in a glass that had thick sides and an upraised bottom, the better to give the illusion that it had more liquid than it did. Fontaine took a sip and surveyed the card-playing area of the Aces Up.

The six tables occupied most of the interior of the place. Two tables were going at the moment, one with five players and one with six. Each table had a dealer as well. Fontaine let his eyes drift, not resting for long on a single player. He wondered if any one of them was Harold Wilson. A couple of them looked capable of killing two men in a roadhouse, but for all he knew, the mousiest one among them, a skinny chap with a nervous mustache and plastered-down hair, could be the man.

Fontaine picked out a person who looked like an employee. He wore a cloth cap with a visor, and he moved from the card tables to the bar. As he stood waiting for an order, Fontaine caught his eye.

The man came over. "Yes, sir?"

"There's a man I'd like to meet who I've been told comes in here on occasion."

The man in the visor showed no expression as he said, "What's his name?"

"Harold Wilson."

"He's in here now." The man motioned with his head, and the visor moved. "That's him at the second table, sitting to the right of the dealer."

Fontaine had not taken notice of the man before, but he did now. Wilson was an average-sized man with a light complexion and a trimmed mustache. He wore a round-brimmed plainsman's hat with a round, rising crown that looked like a bullet head. "Thanks," said Fontaine.

"Would you like me to give him a message?"

Fontaine took his eyes away from the table. "If you don't mind."

"Not at all. We don't care to have bystanders around the game anyway."

"Of course." Fontaine flickered another glance at Wilson and said, "You could tell him I've got a little business matter that I'd like to talk about if he's got a minute." As an afterthought he said, "My name wouldn't mean anything to him, but if he asks where I'm from, you can tell him I come from Redwillow, up by the Dunstan Buttes."

"I'll do that."

Fontaine gave the man a quarter. "Thanks. I appreciate it."

"My pleasure."

A couple of minutes later, Fontaine let his eyes wander. He rested them long enough to see the man in the visor bent down at Wilson's right. Fontaine turned away so he would not be seen looking.

Long minutes passed by. Fontaine made his whiskey last, but even at that he was close to the bottom of his glass when he saw a man next to him in the mirror. He turned to face the man he had asked to meet.

Up close, Harold Wilson was a hard-looking man of about forty. From his expression, one would expect to see lumps or scars, but he had a clear complexion, almost sallow. He had brown hair and brown eyes, all of a tone with his mustache. He was otherwise clean-shaven. He did not wear a vest but rather a shirt with pockets, and the tag from a tobacco sack hung out on his left side. On his right, beneath the collar at the base of his neck, a wine-colored birthmark was visible. He put his hand in his trousers pocket and muttered, "Murphy said you wanted to talk to me."

"Can I buy you a drink?"

Wilson gave him a looking-over. "I'll take one."

Fontaine signaled for two drinks, then put out his hand and said, "My name's Jim Fontaine. I come from the Dunstan Buttes country."

Wilson took out his hand and shook. He eyed the drinks when they appeared, then brought his gaze back to Fontaine. "What kind of business did you want to talk about?"

"I didn't know how else to put it, but there have been a couple of strange things happen in Redwillow. One of them might be connected with a couple of men named Penfield and Pomeroy, and their names led me to you."

Wilson gave him another appraising look. "Are you some kind of a lawman?"

"No. Not even a private investigator."

"Then what's your stake in this?"

Fontaine met Wilson's hard eyes. "A young woman I knew was killed." He knew he was stretching the truth, but it was easier than explaining the whole circumstance, which came to the same thing. "My stake is personal."

Wilson pursed his lips and reached for his drink. After he took a taste he said, "Did these other two have something to do with her, then?"

"Not that I know of. But they were mentioned in connection with another woman who might have come to grief. She disappeared in Redwillow a couple of years ago. But enough things have happened, kind of fishy, that there might be something in common."

Wilson drew himself straight up and held his drink at chest height. "Well, you know, Penfield and Pomeroy are dead, so you can't ask them anything." He took a full slug from the glass without taking his eyes off Fontaine.

"That's what I understand. But if they did something up there, they were working for someone else, and that's what I'd like to find out about."

"You think he might be behind this other girl gettin' killed?"

"I don't know, but if he is, I'd like to see him brought to justice. For both of them."

Wilson took another drink and set the glass on the bar. "Well, if you want to talk to me, you need to tell me his name."

Fontaine hesitated. "I don't know if I want to go that far. After all, it's just a supposition."

Wilson scowled. "How far do you expect to get? If you want me to put cards on the table, you go first."

From the man's comment, Fontaine guessed that he had something to share. "All right," he said, in a lowered voice. "The man's name is Aldredge."

"I've heard it before." Wilson twisted his mouth, then pulled out his tobacco sack and opened it. "What did he do? With respect to Penfield and Pomeroy, that is."

Fontaine finished his first drink and pushed the glass away. The bartender appeared on the spot, and Fontaine signaled for him to bring another drink for Wilson. Then he turned and said, "From what I heard, a woman came to town and had a conversation with him. The talk is that she tried to get money out of him. But then she disappeared. No one saw her leave town. These other two birds were there at the time, and they left right afterwards."

"What was her name?" Wilson didn't look up from rolling his cigarette.

"No one seems to know. But they say she was a dark-haired woman who walked with a limp."

"She was."

"That's what I heard."

Wilson looked up with a hard glint in his eye. "No, I'm telling you. She was."

Fontaine's pulse jumped. "You knew her?"

Wilson licked the seam, patted it, and stuck the cigarette in his mouth. It bobbed as he spoke. "I guess I knew her. And that son of a bitch had her killed. And the ones that did it got theirs." He popped a match and lit his cigarette.

Fontaine had to take a breath. When he was steady he said, "Could you tell me her name?"

Smoke drifted up in front of Wilson's face. "Sure I could. It was Judith. Judith Deaver."

Fontaine repeated the name to himself, then said, "I'm sorry."

"What for?"

"Well, for you, and for her."

"Don't feel sorry for me, mister. I can take care of myself." Wilson finished off his first drink, set the glass on the bar, and moved his new drink closer to him.

"I didn't mean it that way. But I gather you had some feeling for her, and I'm sorry for your—"

"Let's leave feelings out of it." Wilson turned and made a spitting sound, as if he was getting rid of a fleck of tobacco.

Fontaine shrugged. "So you're sure these other two did it?"

"Sure? You're damn right I am. I got Pomeroy by himself, and I got it good and clear out of him. I had to put a little pressure on him. But they didn't like me knowing, so the two of 'em tried to get me up there at Horse Creek. Their mistake." Wilson reached for the full glass and took a drink. He stood with his cigarette in one hand and the glass in another.

"Would it be too much to ask why she went to see Aldredge?"

"Not at this point. I doubt that it'll do much to help this case, though." Wilson squared his shoulders as he sniffed. He took a drag on his cigarette and said, "Here's how it was. Judith had been in a line of work. And she knew of another girl in that line who was strangled. This was in Olathe, Kansas. Judith got on to who did it, the last man who was with that girl. But he hightailed it. Changed his name, moved around. Then she saw him here in Cheyenne, found out his new name, where he lived, and all that. She also found out he had money, and she thought she could get some of it for herself. I was out of circulation at the time, but she came to visit me and told me about it. I told her not to go by herself, to wait till I got out, but she didn't want to wait that long." He drank from his glass. "When I didn't hear from her again, I knew something went wrong. Not that I learned it all at once. But over a period of time, always worrying, I figured it out." He gave a slight shake of the head. "So when I got out, I went looking. I found another girl who knew her, and I heard from another kind of grapevine that Penfield and Pomeroy might have done that job." He lifted his cigarette and paused.

Fontaine took his turn to speak. "She's buried out there, isn't she?"

"I guess it's not that hard to figure out, but how did you know?"

"Aldredge has been trying to buy up several smaller pieces of land, including the one I've got. All in the same area. And someone, whether he knows it or not I'm not sure, has been out there pokin' in the ground with an iron rod."

Wilson nodded as he took a drag.

Fontaine went ahead. "So the evidence has been there all this time, and he doesn't know where it is so he can try to get rid of it."

"That's right. They did it at night. A place where a draw comes down between two hills. Why, hell, by daylight you see a dozen of 'em, and they all look the same."

"Pomeroy told you that much?"

"Oh, yeah. And they wouldn't go back out there during the day." Wilson took a drink and added, "Cowards, all of 'em."

"Have you not thought about going up there and trying to hold him accountable?"

"Of course I've thought of it, but I don't have an idea yet about how to deal with him personally."

"How about in a public way? Bring the law down on him."

Wilson waved his hand. "Ah, all I've got is what I've been told. It's hearsay, and my word isn't worth much. I'd rather do it my way, but like I say, I don't have a plan yet."

"If we had proof, we could try it in the public way."

"You mean find her."

"Well, yes. That might help get justice for her." Fontaine paused. "She deserves that, just like this other girl does."

Wilson tipped his head and looked down as he smoked his cigarette close. As the cloud went up, he said, "I got some justice for her already. It we could hang the son of a bitch behind it, that would help, too."

"I'll tell you, if you come to Redwillow, I'll do whatever I can."

Wilson stepped on his cigarette butt and looked at the drink in his hand. "I might do that. I just might." The conversation had hit a lull, but he did not seem to be in a hurry to get back to his game.

Fontaine picked his own drink off the bar. "Here's to Judith," he said.

In spite of his earlier insistence to leave feelings out, Wilson seemed to be moved, if not by the memories at least by the whiskey. "Here's to her," he said, lifting his glass. "She was a good girl. You know, she broke her leg earlier in life, before I met her, but it never broke her spirit, and she never lost her good looks."

Fontaine drank. For a fleeting few seconds Judith came alive for him. Then she was dead again, and he was thinking of a detail. A mended bone would help identify her.

CHAPTER NINE

Clouds were gathering over the Dunstan Buttes as Fontaine rode back to his cabin. He could smell moisture on the breeze as he unsaddled his horse and put his things inside. The air in the cabin was warm, so he left the door open as he put the buckskin out to graze.

He stood a few yards away from the cabin and faced the breeze as it came across the plain from the buttes. He was glad to be back at his own place and to see that nothing had been disturbed while he was gone. At the same time, he had a sense of impending circumstances, unfinished business. Somewhere out here in this rolling grassland was a cache of guilt that Aldredge wanted to find. If he found it before anyone else did, he stood a chance to get away with murder; if someone else found it first, things might blow wide open.

Fontaine shifted, and with the wind on the side of his face he gazed toward town. As the landscape settled in his sight, a horse and rider materialized. The range was flatter there than it was where it sloped down from the buttes, but even a gentle dip in the land could conceal men and horses and cattle. This rider must have ridden through a low spot.

The clouds in the west made for dull light, and it took Fontaine another minute to see that the rider was Walt Mc-Clatchy. He was still a mile away, so Fontaine relaxed and waited. The horse moved onward, a little faster now as it turned one way and another on its way through the sagebrush and cactus.

McClatchy waved when he came within a hundred yards, then slowed the horse and covered the last thirty yards at a walk. He came to a stop and put both hands on the saddle horn.

"Hullo. Ha'n't seen you in a while."

"I was gone."

"That's what I figured. But I knew you weren't workin' for Gus."

"I took a ride to Cheyenne. Had some business to tend to."

"You haven't had any trouble with your title, have you?"

"Oh, no."

"I didn't think so. I thought you told me you had it all clear. So I didn't know what you were gone for."

"Just a personal matter. Nothin' serious."

"Oh, uh-huh."

"You knew I wasn't workin' for Aldredge, then."

"Oh, yeah. Not sure why. But I heard it."

"Well, I'll tell you. Barrett picked a fight with me because he said I was askin' too many questions."

"Don't know why he's so touchy."

"Neither do I, but I asked the question to you, and the next thing I know, the swamper in the Old Clem has heard it, and Barrett has heard it, and I don't know who-all else has."

"I told you I'd find out what I could."

"Well, that's fine. I appreciate it. But you don't have to repeat every little part of it, like my name."

McClatchy sulked and said nothing.

"Did you happen to hear anything about it yourself?"

"Nothin' new." McClatchy raised his hand and scratched his nose. "Just tryin' to do you a favor."

"Oh, that's all right. I don't know if any more will come of it." Fontaine took on a more cheerful tone. "Anything else new?"

McClatchy shook his head. "Nah."

"Nothing? I've been gone for a week."

McClatchy's nose twitched, and he rubbed it again.

"Oh, well. I'll be goin' into town myself. Maybe I'll hear something." Fontaine looked at the sky to the west. "Looks like we might get some rain."

"Maybe one little thing," said McClatchy.

"What's that?"

The dark blank space in McClatchy's mouth showed as he spoke. "Barrett and Call didn't go to work on the roundup crew after all. Gus pulled 'em and hired a couple other fellas that come through."

"He pulled them?"

"Kept 'em here. I guess he's got things for 'em to look after around here."

"Is that a habit of his, changing things?"

"That's just Gus. You've got to know him."

"I guess so." Fontaine felt a small drop on the side of his face. He turned and felt a couple of more. "Startin' to sprinkle," he said.

"I'd better get goin'." McClatchy leaned forward, then sat back. "What are you gonna do next?"

"What do you mean?"

"Are you gonna go someplace else and work? I thought maybe that was what you were doin'."

"No, I think I'll stay here. Work on my own place. I should probably build a corral."

"I can tell you where you can find a good stand of poles. Yours for the cuttin'. Then when you want to haul 'em, we can use my wagon."

"That's an idea. Thanks."

"Don't cost nothin'. I know what it's like when you're startin' out." McClatchy lifted his head and squinted at the thin drops of rain. "Well, I'd better get goin'. It can open up and rain buckets."

"Good enough. Thanks for stoppin' by."

"You bet." McClatchy settled his hat on his head, stood up in the stirrups, and left on a trot. Twenty yards out, he put the horse into a lope.

Fontaine went to stand in the doorway of his cabin. As the light rain continued to fall, he studied the area close by and thought about the best place to put in a corral.

The rain drizzled through the night. The morning broke clear and made for a pleasant world to look out on. The grass was moist, but the ground was not soaked, and as Fontaine stepped outside he saw that the little dam had collected nothing. A lone antelope stared at him from a half-mile away, and the sound of a meadowlark carried on the clean air.

He used the last scraps of firewood to boil some coffee in a can. When he was done with it and had shaken out the grounds, he had mulled things over. He needed to go to town. Although he always had an accurate idea of how much money he had, he had counted it the evening before, just to be sure. He was not yet close to the green, as card players said, but he needed to be as careful as he could without seeming cheap. Moreover, he needed to buy an ax. Until he found a job that paid, he could work on his own place, and as McClatchy had said, cutting corral poles would cost him only the labor. He could keep himself occupied, learn what he could about developments in town, and be on hand if anything came up. If Wilson did not show up within a week or so, he would start a search himself.

In town he went first to the mercantile, where he looked again at the single- and double-bit axes. Out of a sense of economy he bought a single-bit ax and a leather scabbard for the head. Before he put on the cover, he pressed the heel of his hand against the flat side of the ax head. As he didn't have a collection of tools, he might get some use out of this side as well, such as driving in stakes or even hammering nails.

With his new purchase in hand, he expected to bump into Aldredge on the sidewalk, but he made it to his horse without incident and tied the ax onto the side of his saddle. From there he led the horse down the street to the Inland Sea Café. The sun had climbed past midmorning, and he hoped to find Nora not very busy between the breakfast and noon crowds.

The same two men who had been drinking coffee on an earlier occasion were there again. They both looked at him and went back to their conversation.

Nora came out of the kitchen, flushed and with perspiration on her upper face. A few strands of hair had worked loose, and she looked harried. Her face relaxed when she saw Fontaine.

"Good to see you back," she said.

"I got in to my place yesterday evening, and then it started to rain. Not much, but enough to keep me at home."

"I'm sure you were tired as well."

He lifted his eyebrows as he smiled. "Not that tired. It was more the rain."

She returned the smile. "Bad weather may keep the fleet at anchor."

"Not always bad."

"Depending on who's aboard."

One of the men at the table looked around.

Fontaine motioned with his head toward her and the kitchen beyond. "Looks like you're busy," he offered.

"I've got a mountain of potatoes to cut up. Gertie's making potato soup. She does the onions, though."

"That's good." In a lower voice he said, "Shall I come back

this evening?"

Her eyes had an encouraging shine. "If it doesn't rain."

"I might anyway. At the usual time?"

"That should be fine."

She went back to the kitchen, and he walked to the door. The two men quit talking until he reached the door and opened it. Outside, he untied his horse and turned it so that the new leather scabbard caught the sunlight. With a glance he saw that the man facing the window was watching. To make it worth the man's while, Fontaine grabbed the saddle horn with both hands and swung aboard without putting his foot in the stirrup. Then he put his spur to the buckskin and took off at a gallop.

Nora had a fresher look that evening when Fontaine called for her. Her complexion was clear and dry, and her hair hung loose to her shoulders. She wore a lightweight, light-blue dress with white borders. In her left hand she carried a woman's straw hat with a wide brim and a domed crown. She raised it above waist level and said, "It's not too windy for this, is it?"

He held his own hat at his side and was glad he had taken it off. "Just a hint of a breeze," he said.

"Sailor's delight." With a soft melody she sang, "There's wind in my canvas."

Outside, as she settled the hat onto her head, she seemed to have a bit of the poetic spirit remaining. She said, "Is there a way we can go that we won't have to traverse the whole town? Just for a change, you know."

"I suppose we could walk to the creek. It's not far away. If the wind comes up too strong, we can hurry back without much trouble."

"Tack with the mainsail. Let's give it a try."

"We'll go this same way, then." He led her around the corner, and they walked along the south edge of town.

"Tell me about your trip," she said.

"Uneventful, some of it. Long ride there. I found my old pal, who has a café just as he said he would. Maybe a notch lower than this one, but tolerable all the same. Not long after I got there, I asked about the two men in question."

"Penfield and Pomeroy."

"Right," he said, looking to either side. "And I found out they had, um, come to an end a little while back. They had a run-in with a hard case of a fellow. I had the pleasure of meeting him. You know, I think I'll wait till we get to the edge of town to give names and details." He motioned with his hand. "It's right up here, and we turn left."

The brim of her hat moved as she nodded in agreement.

"In the meanwhile," he said, "is there any news from here?"

"Let's see. Well, yes. Charley Drake got out of jail. I believe that happened after you left."

"Oh. I didn't know that. I saw Walt McClatchy yesterday evening not long after I got back, and he didn't mention it. Maybe it was old news by then."

"I don't think it made much of a stir."

"Anything else?"

"Not that I can think of. Mr. Aldredge's two men are still around."

"McClatchy did tell me that. I suppose Call is still . . ."

"Showing his gallantry. After a fashion."

Fontaine was satisfied with her tone. "Any arrivals or departures?"

"Nothing significant that I've heard of."

They came to the end of the block and crossed the street. To fill in conversation for the next block, he said, "I bought an ax."

"In Cheyenne?"

"No, here. Earlier in the day."

She took a second to answer. "I suppose everyone needs one.

Regular households, that is, and especially in the country."

"I'm planning to cut poles for a corral. Keep me busy. Give a nice show of minding my own business."

"I see."

"I need to be working on my own place anyway."

"Of course."

"Don't worry," he said. "I'm not getting off this other track at all."

"Oh, no. And I'm curious to know the rest of your story."

"Right ahead."

They walked the rest of the block in silence and reached the eastern edge of town. The street that ran north was little more than a worn path between the scattered houses on the left and the grassland on the right. They crossed the street and walked on the shortgrass prairie.

"Back to the story," she said.

"Yes. All about Penfield and Pomeroy. As I said, they came out second-best in a shootout. It happened at a place called Horse Creek, which is little more than a way station on the road north out of Cheyenne toward Iron Mountain and Chugwater. I got the name of the fellow who did 'em in, Harold Wilson, and I found him in a place where he plays cards. The story I got from him seems to be pretty straight."

Her hat brim waved as she nodded for him to go ahead.

"He knew the woman who disappeared here. Her name was Judith Deaver, and they were companions. She had a line of work, as he put it, and he apparently had some other line himself that landed him in the pen for a while. I believe she was in Cheyenne; the penitentiary is in Laramie. Somewhere along the way, she caught sight of Aldredge and recognized him from an earlier time in Olathe, Kansas." Fontaine glanced around and continued his story. "A girl in her line of work had been strangled there, and this woman knew who the last man was that the girl was with. He had a different name then. He took off, changed his name, moved around. Then she saw him in Cheyenne. She found out his new name and where he was living. She also found out he had money, and she thought she could squeeze some out of him. She told Wilson, who told her to wait until he got out, but she didn't want to wait that long. Look out, that's an anthill."

They walked around the mound of granules. Fontaine made sure again that there was no one within hearing distance, and he went on with his account.

"So she came here on her own, and sure enough, Aldredge had Penfield and Pomeroy do away with her. The trouble is, they buried her at night, and afterwards no one was sure whose land it was on. So Aldredge has been trying to find it, and protect it, ever since."

"Should it be that hard?"

"If you don't know the country, and it's at night, one hill looks like another. I guess they didn't follow directions very well, and they couldn't give a clear location afterwards." He paused to think of how to explain it. "They measure land by the section, you know—a square mile—and portions of that. Half-section, quarter-section. There are at least half a dozen parcels out there, and just from the description these fellows gave, she could be on any one of them."

"So that's what some of this strange activity has been about."

"Some of it."

"And how much does this man Wilson know?"

"Some. I'm not sure how much, but more than a little bit. When he got out of prison, which I gather was not that long ago, he went looking. By then he hadn't heard anything from Judith, and he had an idea that things had gone bad. From people at his level, he found out about Penfield and Pomeroy. He squeezed one of them by himself—Pomeroy—and got the story out of him. Then the two of them came after him, and as he said, that was their mistake."

"So where does that leave us?" she asked.

"Well, we could join the search, but I would just as soon not jump right in. For one thing, Wilson said he might come to town. With what he knows, things might happen faster."

Nora gave him a puzzled look. "This is all good and fine," she said, "but how much of this is our case?"

"That's the other thing, and I don't know how to find it out. But I wonder if Emma, in any way, was trying to do what Judith tried."

Nora stopped and faced him with a fallen expression. "I would have to be pretty cold to believe that."

He held her with his eyes. "I know she's your sister, and I don't want to insinuate anything. I don't want to put her on the same level as these other people, but I think you and I have both felt that there's some connection between the two cases."

"Oh, yes. I agree."

"The connection may be only that the same person is responsible but for two different reasons. Or the reasons may be related."

"But she was strangled, like the girl in Kansas."

"That helps us believe he did it. But why? Maybe just out of a compulsion, if that's why he did it before, but maybe to keep someone quiet. And this time he didn't want to leave it to someone else to bungle the job."

Nora's chest rose and fell as she gathered her words. "I have a hard time believing that Emma would do something like that."

He touched her arm. "So do I, at least for your sake. But we can't refuse to consider the possibility."

Nora's eyes were moist. She blinked once, twice. "I know. We can't do anything for her if we don't want to know the truth."

"And maybe the truth isn't bad. Let's try this. Is there any way she might have known this woman Judith?"

"I don't know. I suppose it's possible."

"Was she ever in Cheyenne?"

"I don't know for sure. I wasn't always apprised of where she went. But she could have. After all, Cheyenne is on the main route from North Platte westward and from Denver north. I went through Cheyenne to get here."

"And we don't know how she ended up here."

Nora shook her head and lowered it. "No, we don't." She raised her head, brushed her eyes, and began walking again.

Fontaine kept pace alongside her. The creek was up ahead, and the branches of the red willows were visible where the stream made its oxbow.

They walked to the edge of the bank and stopped. Below them, a few yards away, the clear water flowed over the pebbles. What little breeze there had been had died, and the water looked refreshing.

"Would you mind doing me a favor?" she asked.

"Not at all. What is it?"

She pulled a white handkerchief out of her sleeve. "If you could dampen this."

"Sure." He took the handkerchief, went down the bank, and knelt by the water's edge as he soaked the light cloth. He gave it a squeeze and brought it back to her.

"Thank you." She folded it twice, then dabbed it on her brow and cheeks. "I'm sorry to seem so delicate."

"Nothing to worry about."

"I'm actually rather rugged," she said, in a tone that had a trace of irony. "I've used an ax before. To split kindling. And I can carry water two buckets at a time." She put on a smile. "I could be quite a squaw."

He smiled back. "Oh, I'm sure. But I must say, you look

rather pretty as you are." He touched the back of his right hand to her left.

"Thank you. I'm afraid I let things catch up on me there, but I believe I'm over it now."

"Everything's fine."

He observed her face as she gazed off in the distance, pensive. The rippling stream made a peaceful background sound, and her features softened. He moved closer, she turned toward him, and they met in a soft, brief kiss.

As they drew apart she said, "I wonder if this is how we spend our whole lives. Trying to figure out how things go wrong."

"We're lucky to have the chance."

"I know." After a couple of seconds she said, "Shall we go back?"

"We might as well." He took another look at her with her straw hat, her dark hair to her shoulders, the flowing water in the background, and the red willows growing in the oxbow. "I meant what I said about how pretty you are."

"Thank you. I'm afraid I'm not the most cheerful company right now."

"It's all right. I know we have things to do."

After a minute of walking in silence, she spoke. "Now that I think of it, there was something else I had in mind to say this evening. I got a bit sentimental there, but I think I'm all right."

"Go ahead."

She took a couple of more steps as if she was forming her words. "It has to do with my own story. You know, I told you the main part of it earlier, how I seemed to be repeating the tendency of my mother to marry unreliable men. I don't think I put it in exactly those terms, but that's how I have come to see it."

He nodded for her to go on.

"After those two disasters, a few years later, I developed a mutual interest with a man who was married. We fell in love. It seemed like the real thing, but he had a wife—no children. He told me dreadful stories about her, how she had fits of anger, went on tirades, drank in secret. He said he was putting together a case for legal separation from her. It would just take a little time. So we went on, meeting in all the ways and places that people do. This doesn't sound good, does it?"

"Don't worry. I assume it's all in the past."

"Oh, indeed it is. Anyway, from time to time he had a new reason for a delay—his lawyer needed more information, papers needed to be re-filed, and so forth. We went through two cycles, or rather two phases that each led up to a crisis—one when his wife found out about me, and another, a year later, when she gave him an ultimatum. I learned that he hadn't been working on a case. He intended to, but he couldn't get up the nerve."

"That's too bad, for you to have been led on."

"In the end, he turned out to be a short-changer. He couldn't follow through with what he said he was going to do, which I suppose is understandable, but he didn't have the fortitude to make amends or—resolve things in a decent way. He just left me to work it out on my own terms, which I did. It was no small thing. It rather tore my life apart." She took a deep breath. "So, for all my desire to do something different with my life, I saw that he was not all that different from the first two."

"Unreliable, to use your word."

"Yes, and a fraud in his own way. In spite of seeming bold, which I'll grant he was at times, when it came right down to it, he avoided confrontations. He didn't have it."

"Well, as you said earlier, it's part of what you learn as you go through life."

"Oh, yes." After a pause she looked up. "I appreciate your listening to me. I realize I've given you only a general outline."

He waved his hand. "It's up to you to decide how much of

something to tell, or whether you want to tell anything at all."

"I know. I didn't have to tell this. But I thought it was something you should know before you proceed any further."

He addressed the topic in the terms he thought she meant. "It's not going to influence whether I stick with this case. I'm going to follow through on it."

"I know that, but when we're done with all of this, I wouldn't want to have withheld anything—about myself, or my character, when some of these others seem so dubious."

"I have to say I admire your courage. And what you tell me doesn't trouble me. Everyone's got a past, and they're not all rosy. As for myself, I think I've told you the worst. If anything, I should worry that you might see me as being like the two light-fingered fellows you told me about the first time."

She laughed. "Oh, no. You're different. You don't do something and pretend you don't or didn't. You say you want to be done with those ways, and I believe you. And unlike the third one, you don't say you're going to do something and then stall."

He smiled. "I guess I'm not that hard to figure out. You shouldn't be in for any surprises."

They stopped and turned toward each other as if in unspoken agreement, and they met in a kiss a little longer than the first one. He felt that in the interval he had passed a great test.

When they returned to the front steps of the lodging house, Nora seemed as composed as she was before the discussions of her sister and then herself. Fontaine took off his hat and thanked her for the evening's walk. She took off her hat and fanned her face.

"I'll ask a question I asked earlier," she said. "Where does that leave us?"

"With respect to—?"

"With respect to whether Emma knew anything. I realize we have to try to find out."

"Oh." Fontaine saw that they were back on the main track. "I suppose we would start with someone who knew her, but I think we would have to go about it very carefully, so as not to tip our hand."

"And that someone would be an individual who just—"

"Got out of jail," said Fontaine in a low voice.

"And if that leads nowhere?"

Fontaine hesitated. "Again, I don't like to make unflattering suggestions, but there's another man who claims to have known her, at least according to Charley Drake."

Nora's hat went still. "Who's that?"

Still in a low voice, Fontaine said, "Ray Toomel."

"The one you described as a vermin?"

"I don't remember using that term, but it fits."

"Oh, dear," she said. "I have to brace up and keep myself from saying, or even thinking, that I just can't believe thus and such."

"In this case, I can't believe it, but as I said before, we can't refuse to consider possibilities."

"Leave no stone unturned."

"Correct. Even if all you find is a grub all by itself. Or a dead centipede."

CHAPTER TEN

Fontaine found Charley Drake in the Pale Horse Saloon. Except for having gotten sunburned after being locked up for a month, the young man looked the same as before, in his range-rider clothes, red bandanna, and tall-crowned, light-colored hat.

"Hey, Jim!" he called. "It's you. What do you know?"

"Never very much. How are you doing, Charley?" Fontaine shook his hand.

"Glad to be out, I'll tell you that." Charley turned to the bottle of whiskey sitting on the bar in front of him. "Gimme a glass," he called to the bartender. Then back to Fontaine with a broad smile, he said, "A drink on me, pal. I appreciate you comin' to see me when I was in the pokey."

Fontaine made a smile. "Thanks."

A glass appeared, and Charley poured three fingers of whiskey. "So tell me what you're up to. Walt said you went to Cheyenne."

"I did. Just a little personal business. Now I'm gettin' ready to do some work on my place."

"Oh, yeah. Walt said you wanted to cut some poles."

"He said he knew of a place where there were quite a few."

"I know where it is. I've been there, in fact. It's over on White Creek."

"That's where I get my water."

"I suppose you go straight south?"

"Sure. That's the closest."

"Well, this would be about a mile upstream from there. Good stand of cottonwoods. Lots of young, straight ones." Charley made a circle with his two hands almost touching. "This big around."

"That's good."

"I'll tell you. I should be cuttin' some poles, too. Here's what we can do. I'll help you cut yours. We can haul 'em in Walt's wagon. Then you help me cut mine. I help you build your corral, you help me on mine. Trade labor."

Fontaine wondered about the rush of friendship, but the plan sounded reasonable. "Do you have an ax?" he asked.

"Oh, yeah. I need to sharpen it, but it's fine."

"That's good. I just bought one for myself."

"Oh, hell, we're in business, then. Here. Drink your drink."

Fontaine took a sip. "To begin with, I suppose all we need to do is ride over there and start cutting. After a day or two, we can get the wagon."

"That's right. We'll ride over together. That's not a bad idea, you know. You get anywhere off the beaten path, you're better off in company." Charley gave a confidential look. "This thing ain't over yet, you know. And I've got my ideas about who might be wrapped up in it." He took a drink and lifted an eyebrow. "I thought maybe that was why you went to Cheyenne. Find out about some of those things you were askin' me about."

"Did you know Penfield and Pomeroy were dead?"

Charley put his tongue between his lips, then frowned and said, "I believe I heard something about that, maybe a couple of months back."

"Can't get any information out of someone who's dead."

Charley's brow tightened again. "I thought you went to Cheyenne on personal business."

"I did. I had to talk to the old man I bought my property from. While I was at it, I picked up this other bit of news. New to me, anyway."

Charley gave a short laugh. "I'll tell you about those two. There was a joke about 'em when they were here. One was skinny, and one was fat. Everyone said that if the two of 'em got stranded out in the desert and had to stand in one another's shadow, they would both die. Pomeroy would die first because he couldn't get any shade out of Penfield, and then Penfield would die because his source of shade was gone."

"Well, they're both dead now."

"Any idea who got 'em?"

"Someone they shouldn't have started trouble with, I'd guess." Fontaine tossed off the rest of his whiskey. "I've got to be goin', Charley. Thanks for the drink."

"Don't you want another?"

"I'd better not. I need to go home. When would you like to start that work?"

"Oh. Cuttin' poles? Any time."

"Tomorrow?"

"Sure. I'll be by in the morning."

Charley showed up in the morning as agreed. He had his ax tied across the back of his saddle with the head wrapped in burlap and tied with twine. His eyes showed evidence of his having been out the night before, but his voice was steady. He said he couldn't find his file and hadn't been able to sharpen the blade of his ax. When Fontaine said he didn't have a file, Charley said he would get along with the ax as it was.

They struck off across country to the southwest. After they had ridden about a mile, Fontaine asked if they weren't getting close to some of Aldredge's land.

"He starts just a little farther west," said Charley. "There's a couple of other homesteads we'll be going past."

"Has he tried to buy them out, too?"

"Not that I know of, but he may have."

Charley led the way south around a grassy ridge. Over the next rise, he pointed to a layout that looked like a camp. A tent sat amidst an array of lumber piles, wooden casks, and a couple of wagons with the tongues resting on the ground. Beyond the camp, two men were working with a team of horses and a dirt scraper.

As Fontaine rode closer, he saw that the tent was patched and the stacked lumber was used and weathered. One of the men led the horses and scraper aside, and the other man took up a shovel and began to dig.

"Hello, Adam," Charley called out.

The man with the shovel answered with a syllable that sounded like "Yo."

The other man spoke to the horses and left them standing as he walked over to the excavation. Both men had dark beards, and they looked like brothers.

Charley stopped his horse and leaned on the swells of his saddle. "Whatcha buildin'?"

Fontaine stopped as well.

"Root cellar," said Adam.

"Is that where you hide when the Apaches come for you?"

"Got no Apaches here," said the other man. "It's a place to put spuds. And meat in warm weather."

Adam rested his shovel. "Do you know my brother, Al?" he said.

"Pleased to meet you. I'm Charley Drake. This here's Jim Fontaine."

Al nodded and went for a pick that leaned against one of the wagons.

"We're goin' to cut poles," Charley said.

"Don't cut 'em all." Adam took another shovelful and said, "We want to get some good ridgepoles."

"Oh, there's always more." Charley wagged his head. "You be careful about whose beef you hang in there."

Adam did not stop digging. "You're full of jokes today, Charley. We eat antelope and stay out of trouble."

"Good way to be. Have Aldredge's men come by?"

"Not much. We're not very interestin'." Adam stood aside as his brother swung the pick.

"I suppose that's good, too. Well, we'd better move along. Good to see you, Adam, and good to meet you, Al."

Al raised his head in acknowledgment, and Adam said, "You bet." He shifted his gaze. "And what was your name?"

"Jim Fontaine."

"That's right. Well, it's good to meet you."

"Likewise. And you, too, Al."

Al gave a toss of the head as he stood with the pick in his hands.

Charley clucked to his horse. "We'll save some fat ones for you."

Fontaine swung his ax straight down and cut off the narrow end of the fallen cottonwood.

"That's ten," said Charley. "Why don't we take a rest?"

Fontaine tipped back his hat and wiped the sweat off his forehead. "Not a bad idea." He leaned his ax against a standing tree. Green-leafed branches lay all around, with the fresh-cut poles on top. Fontaine walked to the edge of the grove, where the breeze felt good on his sweaty face. He sat on the ground, and Charley dropped down beside him.

"Lotta work to this," said Charley. "Even after we cut all these, we've still got to peel 'em."

"If it's not one kind of work, it's another."

"Isn't that the truth. How about those two diggin' a cellar?"

"That's work, for sure. I wonder if they're going to grow their own spuds. That'll take water, at least in this climate."

"Seems like a hard way to feed yourself," said Charley. "Knockin' over an antelope, or better yet a big fat deer, seems a lot easier."

Hoofbeats caused both of them to look up and around. Less than a hundred yards to the northwest, a small group of riders came down the bank. As the horses bunched and then separated, Fontaine counted two men and a third trailing. He recognized Barrett and Call right away, but it took him a few more seconds to identify Ray Toomel.

"Son of a bitch," said Charley. "I didn't know he was workin' for them."

"Neither did I."

Barrett and Call rode up to within a couple of yards of where Fontaine and Charley sat. Toomel stayed about a horse's length back.

"Look who's here," said Barrett. "We heard some noise down here, and damned if we don't find a couple of busy beavers."

"Just doin' some honest work," said Charley. He craned his neck. "I see you let any old body ride with you."

Barrett held his mouth in a smug expression as his liquid blue eyes roved over the two seated men. "Just doin' some honest work," he said.

"No doubt. At least you've got him ridin' better horses."

"Shouldn't matter to you."

"As long as he stays off other men's property."

"Fence it out," said Call. "Just like we told Ivanhoe here."

"Who's Ivanhoe?"

"A jouster. Maybe we should call him Sullivan, after the boxer." Call raised his head as he looked down on Fontaine. "How about it, Bare Knuckles?"

Fontaine met his gaze. "Did you fellows come to pick another fight?"

Call sneered. "I understand you're the one that picks fights. We don't like you doin' that with someone who rides for our outfit."

"I doubt that he was ridin' for your boss when I met him. I remember the horse he was on. And furthermore, I gave him fair warning."

"Oh, did you?" said Barrett. He swung down from his horse, put his hat on his saddle horn, and stepped forward. "Show me how you did it."

"Have him come over here, and I will."

"Sure. Get up."

"Why don't you stand back and keep it fair?"

"I will."

Fontaine felt that he was stuck. He pushed himself to his feet, and Barrett moved right in. He slammed Fontaine hard on the left cheekbone, then came across and hit him on the right jaw. As Fontaine staggered backward, Barrett stayed on him and hit him three more times. Fontaine's feet went out from under him, and the back of his head bumped on the ground. As he rolled over and tried to push up on all fours, Barrett leaned over him and punched him on the shoulders, the back of his head, his ribs, whatever spot was vulnerable as he ducked and turned. Then Fontaine went over on his side as the weight of not one but two bodies fell on him. The smell of old sweat hung on Barrett like the odor of a boar hog, and the bulk of his body ground Fontaine's head into the dirt. The weight above shifted, and Charley Drake pulled Barrett off to the side.

"Enough of that," said Charley. "I thought you were going to let them fight fair."

The round-muscled man leaned forward with a leer on his face. His hat being gone, the crooked scar showed across the top of his close-cropped head. "Any fight is fair," he said.

"Well, that's enough of this one."

"Sure," said Barrett with a thin smile. "There's always another time." He looked around for his horse, which Toomel was holding for him. As Barrett walked toward the horse, Toomel picked the hat off the saddle horn and handed it to him. Barrett put on his hat, turned the horse so it stood downhill a couple of inches, stabbed his toe in the stirrup, and slapped up into the saddle.

Toomel stood for a moment with his wide eyes staring and his heavy lips parted.

"Let's go," said Barrett. "Leave these girls to their work."

Call stuck out his lower lip, blew a puff of air upward toward his hat brim, and turned his horse to follow the others.

Charley Drake did not show up to work the next morning. After waiting an hour, Fontaine went by himself, figuring that Charley might need to sober up and come along later. Fontaine worked alone the whole day, however, cutting a few more than half the number of poles he and Charley had cut the day before. He kept close count toward the late afternoon, and when he had fifty poles altogether, he wrapped the head of his ax and tied the handle to his saddle.

On his way home, he rode around the base of a low bluff. He had noted the two layers of clay that were exposed on the south and east sides and was watching the swallows dart back and forth when a buckboard wheeled out of the shadows of another hill farther west. He recognized the two palominos, then the shiny tan body of the vehicle, and the man sitting in the shade of the canvas cover. The trail led through the bottom of the grassy swale, so Fontaine waited uphill to let the wagon pass. The palominos trotted by, and Aldredge raised his hand to wave. Fontaine waved back.

Dusk was settling on the range as Fontaine held his hand against the buckskin's shoulder and pulled the latigo. He was still sore from the fight the day before, and he had worn himself out pretty well cutting poles on his own, but he had an uneasy feeling that kept nudging him to go to town. He untied the ax, left it with the shovel inside the cabin, and pulled himself up into the saddle.

Night had fallen by the time he reached town. As he had found Charley Drake in the Pale Horse Saloon the time before, he went there first. Only a couple of men, both unknown to Fontaine, stood at the bar, so he did not linger. He untied his horse, rode to the Old Clem Saloon, and tied up again.

The interior was lit as usual, and the stoop-shouldered man with greying blond hair and a bushy mustache was tending the bar. A few men stood along the bar and sat at tables. The lamp was lit above the poker table in the corner, and a game was under way. Fontaine cast a casual glance upward at the golden eagle, then down again at the card table. Out of habit he counted the players—one, two, three, four, five—and he froze. There at the table on the dealer's right, his face in shadow from his bullet-headed hat, sat Harold Wilson.

Fontaine ordered a beer, exchanged a nod of recognition with the bartender, and laid a silver dollar on the bar. His heartbeat had picked up. He made himself stay calm, told himself there was no need to act too soon. Wilson had settled into a poker game and would be in no hurry. He had most likely come in on the afternoon stage, so he wasn't going anywhere fast.

Fontaine drank his beer at leisure. Every few minutes he caught a glance at the poker table, and nothing changed. Things were slow at the bar as well. The portly man in the dark suit came in through the front door and stood where he had been on the first night Fontaine had come in. Occasionally a voice lifted, and on one occasion Fontaine was reminded of the bartender's name when he heard a man call him Doby. All this time, Wilson showed no indication of having seen Fontaine, though Fontaine was sure that a man of Wilson's caliber would not have failed to notice him.

At length Fontaine decided that Wilson was waiting for him to make the first move, so he left his near-empty mug on the bar and sauntered over to the card table. When the next hand was over and the dealer was gathering in the cards, Fontaine stepped closer and asked, "What kind of game is this?"

"Friendly game," said a man in a clean hat and a neat vest.

The dealer pushed the cards together to make a deck. "Five-card draw," he said. "Dollar limit, five-dollar buy-in, minimum."

Wilson looked up, met Fontaine's eyes, and returned to watch the dealer's handling of the cards.

"Care to play?" the dealer asked.

"Not quite yet. I'll think about it. I'm over at the bar."

"Push the poodgie," said the dealer.

The man in the clean hat moved an oversized wooden chip with a red center, which served as a dealer's chip, to the next player on his left. Wilson did not look up, so Fontaine went back to the bar.

Time dragged on. Fontaine ordered a second beer and took his time to drink it. Wilson did not order a drink or get up from the table. Fontaine went out back, returned to his place at the bar, and was about to order another beer when Wilson pushed his chips toward the dealer and stood up from the table. A minute later, he appeared in the mirror on Fontaine's right.

Fontaine signaled to the bartender and turned to Wilson. "Care for a drink?"

"I'll have one."

The bartender appeared, wiping his hands on a cloth.

Fontaine ordered a beer for himself and a whiskey for Wilson.

"Just get to town today?"

"This afternoon."

"How's the poker game?"

"Slow."

The drinks arrived. Wilson rotated his and set it closer, but he did not drink yet.

"I understand this place is crooked as hell," he said.

"This saloon, or this town?"

"Both."

"Could be."

Wilson turned, took a drink, and rested both forearms on the bar. Fontaine decided to leave him be and let him have his stoic silence. A good fifteen minutes passed without either of them speaking, and Fontaine noticed that Wilson did not drink as fast as he did on the earlier occasion in Cheyenne.

Movement in the mirror caught Fontaine's attention as two men came into the saloon. He was standing on his left foot with his right foot on the rail, and just as he was recognizing the men in the mirror, someone kicked his left bootheel. His leg buckled, and he stood up and turned to face George Call. The man's hat was tipped back and his face was close up, his waxy nose and prominent ears shining in the lamplight.

"Watch out you don't trip someone," he said.

"Who have we got here?" said Barrett. The shorter man stood with his hands on his hips and his elbows out, so that his muscled shoulders stuck forward. "Havin' trouble standin' up, puncher? Seems like that's an old problem of yours."

"Everyone has a problem," said Fontaine.

"Is that right? What's mine?"

"The company you keep."

Barrett smirked and raised his head as he passed the buck to his partner.

"And what's mine?" Call asked.

"I'm sure you don't have any—" Fontaine paused.

Call's face widened with a shiny smile.

"—that you're aware of."

The smile faded. "I'd like to rub your face in the dirt."

Wilson turned from the bar. "Why don't you two shove along? You're irritatin' me."

Barrett's liquid eyes moved and settled. "Are you a friend of his?"

"Not yet."

Barrett's expression stopped, as if he understood something at a level lower than conscious thought. "Well, be careful of the company you keep." Sarcasm came back to his face as he said, "So long, puncher."

When Barrett and Call had moved down the bar, Wilson said, "Who are those two yokels?"

"They work for Aldredge."

"So do you have trouble with him?"

"Not outright. Just with them. But it might amount to the same thing."

"I don't like them."

"I'd be surprised if many people did."

"Surprise," said Wilson. "That's what some people need." He turned back to the bar and lapsed into silence as he rolled a cigarette and lit it. He stared at the mirror, ignoring Fontaine and maintaining his study with the help of his cigarette and his whiskey.

He finished the cigarette, smoking it down to his fingernails, then dropped the butt on the floor and stepped on it. Without a word he turned and walked in the direction of the back door.

Fontaine had seen the same kind of strut before—the squaring of the shoulders, the upright carriage, the lift of the chin. Wilson strolled past Barrett and Call and ignored them on his way out back.

As Wilson returned a few minutes later, Fontaine saw the same posture. Barrett had seen it, too, or felt it. He had turned from the bar and stood straight up, rotating his upper body and lifting his head as Wilson walked by. Tension hung in the air, a lethal sensation that Fontaine could feel from twenty feet away.

Wilson took his place at the bar and tossed off the last of his drink. He signaled for another, still ignoring Fontaine, and paid for it himself. Then he lifted a boot onto the rail and leaned on the bar top as he took a slow drink of whiskey.

Barrett and Call set their glasses on the bar, and their voices rose in the tone of someone about to leave. A few seconds later, they began to walk to the front door.

Wilson shifted position, and Fontaine could see him watching in the mirror. Just as Barrett and Call were about to pass behind him, he stood up and moved back half a step. He jostled Barrett, who jerked to the side and bumped into Call.

Barrett squared around. "Hey, buster, watch what you're doin."

Wilson made a slow turn and drew himself up to his full height. He was of average height himself but a few inches taller than Barrett. He said, "You need to watch where you're goin'."

Barrett's liquid eyes took on a blaze. It was evident that he was used to intimidating men with his stare. "Don't tell me what I need."

"I just did."

Barrett's face clouded. "This is twice you've gone too far. I didn't like the way you butted in earlier, and I don't like the way you're talkin' now."

"You don't have to like it."

Barrett smiled. "You'll find out what I like."

Wilson's fist came up and popped Barrett on the cheekbone. The shorter man fell back and bounced forward, and Wilson hit him two more times.

The gravelly voice of the man in the dark suit carried down the bar. "Take it outside, boys."

Doby the bartender appeared. "Just like he said. Take it outside. I count to five, and I get my shotgun."

Barrett's face was full of contempt as he spoke to Wilson. "You hear that? He means it. You started this thing, and if you're man enough, you'll step outside and finish it."

"Fine with me."

A small crowd had gathered, so the two men had a following as they headed for the front door. Barrett went out first, then Wilson, then Call, then Fontaine and a half-dozen others. Both combatants had left their hats inside, and now they stood beyond the sidewalk with their fists raised.

"Move aside and don't block the light," said Barrett.

The crowd parted on the sidewalk, and the light from the open door flowed out.

"Come on," said Barrett.

He took a step to the left, then lunged forward with a quick left jab. He caught Wilson on the jaw, but Wilson came back with two fast punches, one to each side of Barrett's head. That seemed to stop Barrett for a second, and Wilson smashed him in the middle of the face.

Barrett stepped back, blinking, as he held his hand to his nose. Blood showed between his fingers and dripped on his shirt. He sniffled, turned his hand to cup the blood, then covered his nose again. Blood fell in drops to the ground as well as on his clothes.

"I'm going to have to stop," he said. "But we'll pick this up again. Believe me, we will." He studied Wilson, who stood with his fists at waist level.

"Any time," said Wilson.

Call had moved up to Barrett's side. With a resentful look at

Wilson he said, "You're lucky he can't finish you off right now."

"Why don't you try?"

"I don't fight with shit-faced—"

Wilson moved fast. He hit Call once, twice, three times, and laid him out. Call's hat went tumbling, and it took him a few seconds to get up onto one elbow and rub his fingers against the side of his chin.

"You don't fight at all," said Wilson. "You're just a big mouth." He put his hand in his trousers pocket, and Fontaine was quite sure he saw the end of a brass bar disappear.

Doby appeared in the doorway with the two men's hats. "Take these," he said. "That's all for either of you this evening. You two, and the two you were drinking with."

CHAPTER ELEVEN

Fontaine rested his ax and counted his day's work one more time to be sure. Eighteen, just like the day before. He had stacked them six at a time today, to keep easier count. The other stacks, scattered through the grove, ranged from five to a dozen poles. There were still a great many trees standing—far more than the ones lying on the ground. Many were bent at the base and would not have a straight section long enough for a few more years. Many were too thick, as he wanted poles no bigger around than six inches at the wide end.

The two brothers, Adam and Al, should be able to find ridgepoles to their liking. As for the corral poles, once they were peeled and dried, they would all be laid lengthwise, overlapping on the ends, for rails, or they would be cut and fastened together for gates. Cottonwood would not last long for upright posts sunk in the ground. For those, cedar worked the best. Even from a distance he could see that cedars grew aplenty in the Dunstan Buttes. It would be a matter of finding a place where he could cut them.

McClatchy would know. McClatchy knew everything about who had what and what grew where. If he didn't know, he would ask until he found out.

Sixty-eight poles. He was just getting started. They wouldn't last long once he started laying them out for rails. What he had now was probably a wagonload. He guessed he needed at least three loads. Then posts, and at some point he would have to buy hardware. In the meanwhile, it didn't cost anything to work. That was the good thing.

He covered the head of the ax and tied the handle onto the saddle. After leading the horse to the creek and letting him drink, Fontaine mounted up and rode out of the grove. A light breeze cooled the sweat inside his shirt. That didn't cost him anything, either.

Other things did. He was going to have to go into public places to look for Charley Drake again. He wasn't the other man's keeper, but he needed to know whether Charley was going to work. If not, he could have his half of the poles the two of them cut the first day. Or Fontaine could make a deal for them. Trade some other kind of labor.

Maybe Charley didn't like to work. Fontaine realized he didn't know Charley all that well. The topic of Penfield and Pomeroy, for example. Charley had known more than he let on. Then to say he was going to work and not show up. Whether he didn't want to work, had been intimidated, was on a drunk, or had something else come up, Fontaine needed to know. Other people left things hanging, but he didn't.

Fontaine looked for Charley in the Pale Horse Saloon and again did not find him. He hoped to see him early enough to get things resolved and still have time to drop in on Nora. It had been too late the night before, and even more so after having a few drinks and being party to a fight. If he could have one beer and get out early this evening, he would like it better.

He went to the Old Clem Saloon and did not find Charlie Drake there. Although a card game was getting under way, he did not see Harold Wilson, either. He ordered a beer with Doby the bartender. As the man leaned to set the beer on the bar, he looked forward beneath his brows and spoke in a tone of disapproval.

"Your friend's pretty drunk."

Fontaine felt a small jolt of alarm. He did not know whether the bartender meant Charley or Wilson, but neither was good. "Where is he?" he asked.

"He went out back. Unless he passes out in the alley, he should be back in here in a few minutes."

Fontaine sipped on his beer and waited. The portly man in the dark suit came in and took his usual place at the bar. All five card players had chips in front of them, and the dealer was spinning out cards. The back door opened, a couple of men turned to look out of habit, and Charley Drake walked in.

He was carrying himself all right, walking straight with his shoulders up, but it looked as if he was making an effort to do so. His light-colored hat was cocked, and his face was flushed. When he saw Fontaine, his face broke into a smile. He walked right up and clapped Fontaine on the shoulder.

"Well, Jim. What the hell!"

"Evenin', Charley."

Charley stepped back, laid his hand on a glass of whiskey, and scooted it down the bar. Standing a couple of feet from Fontaine and facing him, he leaned his forearm on the bar. He was wearing the same shirt as two days earlier, and his red bandanna was matted and limp. His face was shiny with old sweat, and his chin was stubbled. He smiled with one side of his mouth, as if there was a good joke between the two of them. Then he tipped his head in a gesture of sincerity.

"Good to see you, Jim. Glad you came in."

"Hadn't seen you, and I thought I should find out."

Charley grimaced. "I got sick, is what I did. After sittin' in one place so long, and then goin' out and pourin' it on, workin' and sweatin' and drinkin' a bellyful of water, I got sick." He put his hand on his stomach. "Did somethin' to my guts."

"Uh-huh."

"Oh, I know I shouldn't have drank so much, but that in itself didn't do it. I was home in bed all day yesterday. I barely got back on my feet today."

"Well, I've been able to work without you, so I've gotten by. But I need to know if you want to go back to work on the same deal."

"Oh, yeah. You bet."

"When do you think you can work again?"

"Tomorrow."

Fontaine gave him a close look. "Do you think you'll be straightened out by then?"

Charley frowned and tipped his head back. "Oh, hell, yes. I feel fine now."

"I hope you don't stay out late. Do you think you can get home all right?"

"Sure I can."

Fontaine took a drink, and Charley did the same. Fontaine's eyes wandered toward the card table and back.

Charley spoke. "I guess your friend left town."

Fontaine flinched. "Who's that?"

"Wilson."

"How do you know about him?"

Charley waved with his free hand toward Doby and the others. "They were all talkin' about him. They said he came in here last night, played cards for a while, cleaned a couple of clocks, and left on the afternoon stage."

"North?"

"That's right. Where do you think he went?"

"I have no idea."

Charley tucked his chin. "They said he knows his business."

"I hope he does."

"Maybe he'll stop on his way back."

"Do you know where he's from?"

154

"They said he came in from Cheyenne yesterday." Charley had a slur in his voice. "What do you know about him?"

"Not much. He kept to himself. Stood right here and hardly said anything."

"Well, there's a son of a bitch."

Fontaine frowned, and Charley motioned toward the front door. Fontaine turned to see Ray Toomel in his usual grubby attire of untucked shirt, grimy sagging pants, and clunking boots. The man showed no surprise at seeing Fontaine and Charley as he came shuffling toward them. His eyes were wide and expressionless, his face was stubbled, and his heavy mouth hung open.

As he walked by with the odor of woodsmoke trailing, he said something in a casual tone of greeting. The word sounded like "Pilgrims."

"What was that?" said Charley, in a challenging tone. He stood up, wavered, and rested his hand on the bar.

Toomel stopped. "I said, 'Pilgrims.' "

"And what's that supposed to mean?" Charley took a drink as he looked sideways and glared. "We didn't just get here."

"Pilgrims are travelers," said Toomel.

"And so?"

"I heard you were both leavin'." The wide eyes made a slow pass over the two of them.

Charley took his hand from the bar, teetered, and gained his balance. "I'm not goin' nowhere," he said.

"It's a good thing. You can barely walk."

"There's nothin' wrong with me."

"Hah. Nothin' that another month in the jug wouldn't cure. Dry you out."

Charley's brow grew heavy. "It wasn't fair that I got thrown in to begin with, and I got out clean and honest."

Toomel moved his head back and forth, as if he was taking

Charley's measure. "They should have kept you longer. What did you do all the time you were in there?"

"What's it to you?" Charley's eyelids began to droop. His head gave a jerk, and he forced his eyes open. He swayed on his feet and reached for his drink.

"You probably spent your whole time moonin'. Over your little lost hair pie."

Charley puckered his mouth and sprayed whiskey in Toomel's face. Toomel took it, standing back with a glowering look as Charley said, "Don't you even mention her name. You aren't fit to lick the ground she walked on."

Toomel moved up close. "Lick?" he said, and he pushed Charley backwards. Charley stumbled once and fell, and his hat rolled away. Toomel walked toward him and laid the sole of his heavy boot on Charley's neck and jaw. "Lick?" he said again. "Why don't you lick the floor?"

Fontaine was about to interrupt when Doby came bustling over.

"Look here," said the bartender, "we won't have any of that. You understand?"

Toomel drew back his boot, which Fontaine was sure Doby had not seen. "No one threw a punch," said Toomel. "He's so drunk, he can't stand up."

"You pushed him," Fontaine said.

The bartender, with his head leaning forward as always, rotated in his stiff manner. "Why are you always right alongside?"

"I had no part in this argument. It was between these two. Charley said something this fellow didn't like, so he pushed him down. Took advantage of a drunk."

"Hah," said Toomel, casting a superior look at Charley. "Man talks to me like that, if he was sober he'd get his throat cut."

Fontaine noted that Toomel had neither a pistol nor a sheath knife. Maybe he had a clasp knife in his pocket.

"Now, now," said Doby. "There's no brains in saying something like that."

"At least I'm sober. I haven't even had a drink yet."

"Well, I don't know if I want to serve you."

Toomel raised his head, closed his mouth, looked to either side, and came back to the bartender. "My money should be as good as anyone else's. And I'll even help him up."

He turned toward Charley, but before he bent very far, Fontaine stepped in. "I'll do it," he said.

"Then I'll sit over here," said Toomel. Looking at Doby, he added, "If you think I'm good enough to be served in this place, I'll have a glass of whiskey."

Fontaine reached down and helped Charley sit up. Then he got repositioned and pulled him to his feet.

The portly man in the dark suit appeared, and in his gravelly voice he said, "Here's his hat." He handed it to Fontaine and walked out of the saloon.

The bartender stood at the far corner of the bar, engaged in conversation with a couple of other patrons. Charley was taking deep breaths. His eyes were redder now.

Toomel got up from his chair, walked behind Charley to the bar, and leaned there. Within a minute the bartender served him a glass of whiskey.

Charley turned around, saw Toomel, and turned back. "I'd like to twist his neck."

"Forget about it for right now," Fontaine said. "You're too drunk, and you'll just get thrown out in the street."

"Throw him out in the street."

"You won't do anything of the sort. If you try anything, you'll end up on your ass again."

Charley stood in a daze for a long couple of minutes. His hat was perched on his head, and his eyelids were lowered. He reached for his whiskey and drank the last of it. Just as he was putting the glass down, the bartender set another drink in front of him.

"From Ray. To show there's no hard feelings."

"He's full of shit like a Christmas turkey."

"Do you want it or not?"

"Sure. I'll take it." Charley raised his head and scratched his chin. "Jim, do you want one?"

"No, thanks. I'm goin' to leave pretty soon."

"One more won't hurt you."

"I know, but I need to be goin'." Fontaine reached for his mug and drank part of what was left. Two more swallows and he would be out of the place.

The front door opened, and Fontaine was surprised to see Gus Aldredge walk in. He was wearing a light-colored hat and suit as usual, and he was carrying a small quirt with the thong around his wrist. He was also wearing lightweight leather gloves that looked like deerskin.

He sauntered past Fontaine and Charley, giving a nod of greeting along with the syllable, "Boys." He walked up to Toomel, and in a voice loud enough for Fontaine to hear, he said, "Go to the stable and saddle your horse. There's work to do at the ranch, and you need to be there."

"Tonight?"

"Yes, tonight." He motioned with the quirt. "Finish your drink, and get gone."

"Yes, sir."

Aldredge turned and left Toomel at the bar. On his way to the door he stopped next to Fontaine. He lifted his chin and tipped his head toward Charley. "I'd say your friend needs some looking after."

Charley took his drink off the bar and held it in front of his chest. His mouth was open, and his head did not hold still. "In your ass, you son of a bitch. I know what you're made of."

Aldredge's eyebrows went up, and he walked away.

A couple of minutes later, Toomel went out the front door. He wasn't gone half a minute when the man in the dark suit came back in.

Ah-ha, thought Fontaine. *That's where Aldredge came from.*

Fontaine took his second-to-last drink, waited a few minutes, and finished his beer. He set his mug on the bar. "Are you ready to go, Charley?"

"I'm not done yet."

"Well, when you are, you might think about sleepin' in the stable and goin' home when it's daylight."

"Sure." A smile spread across Charley's shiny face. "Lookin' after your old pal, aren't you?"

"I'll tell the stable man to expect you."

Charley gave a slow wink and a dip of the head.

Fontaine went out the front door and down the block to the corner. Lantern light showed inside the stable. As Fontaine pulled the door open and went in, he caught the closed-in smell of horses and hay and straw. The voice of the stable man sounded as he said, "Yup, yup" to an animal. Fontaine took two more steps and halted.

Lying on a bed of straw, with his hat over his eyes and his mouth open, was the unkempt shape of Ray Toomel.

The stable man appeared with a herding stick in his hand. "What do you need?" he asked.

Fontaine waved his hand at the sleeping figure. "I thought he would be gone."

"He asked me to wake him in fifteen minutes. That was about ten minutes ago."

"Well, I hope he's gone pretty soon. He just had a scrape with Charley Drake, and Charley's too drunk to ride home. I told him he should stay here and I'd drop by to mention it."

"That should be all right. "I'll make sure this one gets out of here."

Fontaine thanked the man and walked back to his horse. Night had fallen, but he didn't think it was ten o'clock yet. Maybe nine-thirty or a quarter till. It shouldn't be too late to call on Nora.

He had swung aboard and ridden less than fifty yards when two gunshots, one right after the other, exploded in the night. His horse spooked, and he reined it in. The sound came reverberating from between two buildings on his left, so he placed the shots as coming from the alley in back. He wheeled his horse around and spurred it. He reached the corner and went around it on a lope, then turned right again into the alley behind the stable. No one was in sight, but he heard voices from up ahead. They would be coming from the back of the Old Clem Saloon.

To keep from getting shot himself, he rode around to the street and went in the front door. A crowd of men had gathered at the back of the saloon, and he heard voices rising and falling as he made his way. When he got there, men moved aside for him. Lying on the floor, with blood staining the front of his shirt, was Charley Drake.

Fontaine knelt by his side. "Who did this, Charley?"

"I don't know. I went out back, and someone must have been waitin' for me."

"Toomel," said one man, and another repeated the name.

The back door squeaked, and Ray Toomel walked in. "Not me," he said. "I was asleep in the stable. The shots woke me up. You can ask the stable man."

Hubbub started in the crowd, and Fontaine looked up at the men standing around. "I saw him there myself. That's not our main worry right now, anyway. We need to help Charley."

Doby the bartender spoke. "You've got to get him out of

here. I can't have him bleedin' all over the place. Someone needs to tell the barber to open his shop."

The man in the dark suit said, "I'll do it."

A few minutes later, the barber appeared with a grey wool blanket. They got it under Charley, and four men including Fontaine lifted him.

"Just a word," said Doby. "Everyone who was here, remember what happened. This'll have to be reported to the sheriff."

They carried Charley out the front door, diagonally across the street, and into the barber shop. The barber led the way to a back room adjacent to the one in which customers took baths. The other three men left, and the barber pulled Charley's shirt up to his chest.

"He's hurt pretty bad. Let me go get some gauze."

When they were alone, Fontaine asked again, "Who did this, Charley?"

Charley was wide awake, like a drunk who had a good scare. "I don't know, but I can guess. Someone who works for Aldredge."

"What for? Because of that last thing you said?"

"I don't remember what I said."

"You told him you knew what he was made of."

Charley smiled and gave a short, broken laugh. "I told him that?"

"Yeah, you did."

"He knew anyway." Charley's body twisted. "Jesus," he said. "They hit me dead center. I'm not going to make it, am I?"

"I don't know."

"It's all my fault."

"Don't blame yourself. Just hang on."

"But it is my fault. Or they would never have done anything to Emma."

"What do you mean?"

Charley's eyes were almost vacant. "Is there just you and me here?"

"Just the two of us."

"Well, I know I'm on the way out, so I might as well tell someone."

"Go ahead."

Charley heaved a breath. "When I was sure about what Penfield and Pomeroy did, I knew I had something on him. I thought I could do something with it, and that would be what I needed to get a new life for me and Emma."

This was it. Charley wanted to get it off his chest, and Fontaine figured he had better take what he could. "Did you use her for bait?"

"It was his weakness. I knew that. He'd been with her a few times. But once I laid the trap, I made sure I was always close by whenever she was with him. Until that last time. I thought the apple was ready to fall, but—" Charley made a gargling sound, and his chest went up and down.

"But what, Charley?"

"Where was I?"

"You said you thought the apple was about to fall."

Charley moved his head. "I don't know. Things are gettin' hazy."

"Here, take my hand." Fontaine felt the pressure, not very strong.

After a few seconds, Charley said, "Who's this?"

"I'm your pal, Jim."

"Sure, Jim. It's dark, you know."

"Sure it is. Just hang on."

Half a minute passed, and Charley's upper body moved. "There's a light now," he said. "Someone's coming." His lips moved without saying anything, and then his voice was clear. "Is that you, Willie?"

Fontaine squeezed, and the pressure in return was faint.

"Willie, by God. You came back."

In the morning, Fontaine rode into town to check with the barber again. "I just want to make sure he gets a decent burial."

"I'll see to it. He had a couple of dollars on him, and that can go toward it. If he had some other put away, or if there's something of his to be sold, that could help as well."

Fontaine met the barber's eyes. The man was impersonal, businesslike. He had to be. "Sure," said Fontaine. "He had another friend, a neighbor. Walt McClatchy. We'll see what we can do between the two of us."

The barber closed his eyes and nodded. Then he said again, "I'll see to it."

Fontaine had a dazed, detached sensation as he went out of the barber shop and stood on the sidewalk. He let out a long breath. It was all over for Charley Drake. He recalled the time he had seen Charley right after he got out of jail. Charley's words came to him now. "This thing ain't over yet, you know." Charley knew why; it was for knowing too much.

Fontaine stepped down from the sidewalk and untied his horse. Now it was his turn. In Aldredge's eyes, he knew too much. Charley's words came back to him again, as if he himself had said them out loud. "This thing ain't over yet."

He stepped into the saddle and turned the horse into the street. As he took in his surroundings and came back to the present moment, he recognized a man riding toward him. It was Walt McClatchy. Fontaine rode forward to meet him, and the two drew rein in the middle of the street.

McClatchy's big hands rested on the saddle horn. His face was shaded by the broad brim of his hat, but a twitch was visible as he spoke. "Heard about Charley," he said.

"I just came from the barber's. He said he would take care of things, but there's a little more money that'll have to be made up. I told him you and I would take care of it, maybe sell something of his if he didn't have any money put by."

"I doubt that he did. You know, he didn't have much except a few cows, which I was lookin' after. We could sell them if we had to. I guess we should. I could buy 'em, as far as that goes."

"We'll see. It doesn't have to be all done today."

McClatchy gave a solemn nod. "Hell of a thing for that fella Toomel to do."

"Oh, I don't think he did it. He was in the stable."

"Not what I heard. The stable man said he didn't see him in there when the shots were fired."

"Then he had a lot of nerve showin' up right afterwards."

"That's what everyone says."

"Has anyone gone after him? Has he gone out to Aldredge's place?"

"I don't know that anyone's done anything. You know how they do. Just wait until the sheriff comes." McClatchy twisted his mouth and sniffed. "They sent for him."

"Well, none of this is any good," said Fontaine. "I think we should go out to his place and take a look. If he's got anything of value there, we don't want someone walkin' off with it."

"You think so?"

"I don't trust any of 'em. Toomel's been workin' for Aldredge, but he's got sneaky ways of his own. And those other two could be up to anything."

"I suppose you're right. I had some other things to do, but I can come back and do them later."

On the way out to Charley's homestead, as they rode along, they fell into conversation about normal things. McClatchy got all of the details out of Fontaine regarding how many poles he had cut, how long they were, how big around, and how long it had taken Fontaine to cut them.

"I think we can get 'em all in one wagonload so they don't sit there. Then if you want to go out and get some more, we'll make a second trip."

"I'm sure I'll need more. A stack disappears fast on a job like this. Before I start building the corral, though, I'll need some posts. I'd like to get some cedar."

"Oh, I can show you where to get 'em. I got mine a couple of years ago. Sixty-six of 'em." He gave Fontaine a confidential smile. "Now those are heavy. I had to make two trips to get 'em."

"There's still some out there?"

"Oh, they're like hair on a dog's back. You wouldn't know I been there. Well, you would if you saw the stumps."

They covered the distance to Charley's place in less than an hour. Fontaine hadn't been to the homestead site itself, so the layout was new to him. A small shack sat on a bare spot of ground with a small pen on one side. A hundred yards back from the house, a row of chokecherry trees grew at the base of a low hill. As he brought his gaze back to the house, he saw a horse in the pen.

"Looks like someone's here," he said. Giving a closer look, he recognized the dull-colored animal with protruding hip bones and a ragged tail. "You know whose horse that looks like."

They rode up to the yard and called out, but no one came to the door. The horse in the pen was saddled and bridled, with the reins knotted and hanging on the saddle horn.

McClatchy looked at Fontaine with his eyes opened wide. "How do you think we should do this?" he asked.

"Why don't you watch the back door, and I'll try the front. If he's got it locked, we might have to ask someone else to help us."

"I can try the front," said McClatchy. "He's got nothin' against me."

"He might feel cornered. Go ahead around back. I'll be careful."

Fontaine dismounted and drew his pistol as McClatchy rode away. The dull-colored horse grunted and turned its head. Fontaine draped the buckskin's reins over the hitching rail and moved toward the door. He and McClatchy had already called out and made plenty of noise, but still he felt the need to be careful. He took light, cautious steps until he reached the door. Standing to one side, he rapped on the door frame.

"Anyone in there?" he called.

No answer.

"If there's anyone in there, you shouldn't be. You'd be better off if you just came out."

Still no answer sounded.

Fontaine tried the doorknob, a dull black porcelain thing, and the door opened. He pushed it until it scraped on the floor. The quietness seemed strange. Fontaine peered into the room as well as he could from where he stood, and he saw something that looked like the bottom of a shoe. Craning his neck further, he saw two feet sticking out beneath a blanket.

With his gun trained on the object, he stepped inside. It looked to be a body beneath a blanket. He told himself to be careful. The body might be holding a pistol and waiting for a close shot.

He went around to the head and stood out of the possible line of fire. The body did not move. Fontaine lifted the corner of the blanket with the toe of his boot, and he brushed against the body. The rigidity told him that the person was not going to move.

Bending down, Fontaine pulled back the blanket and looked into the vacant, staring eyes of Ray Toomel. The man's hat had been underneath the blanket as well. Toomel didn't need it anymore. He had a dark hole in his forehead.

Fontaine covered the body and let out a long breath. He went to the back door and opened it. "Come on in," he said. "He's not goin' anywhere."

McClatchy stepped around the corner of the house with his gun in his hand and a questioning look on his face.

"It's Toomel," said Fontaine. "It looks as if we've got something else to report to the sheriff."

CHAPTER TWELVE

The wind had stopped blowing, and the clouds had gathered with the promise of rain. They rested along the top of the Dunstan Buttes and left the rangeland in shadow. At the northern end of the buttes, the setting sun cast a panel of pink and orange beneath the cloud cover, so that the landscape at that distance was lit up with a bright, uncharacteristic color.

Fontaine waited outside The Gables as Nora went inside. At the last minute she decided not to wear her hat. Now she came out smiling, her dark hair flowing over her shoulders.

"I'll take my own chance at getting wet," she said. "But the hat wouldn't do much good, and the rain would turn it into something like a wet rag. I had one like it before." She looked up at the clouds. "I wish I had an umbrella. With me, that is. I have two in North Platte."

"It's like my slicker. I left it at the cabin."

"Well, let's walk," she said. "I like the place we went to last time."

As they set out, Fontaine said, "If we get soaked, you'll wish we stayed in the parlor."

"Walls have ears. And we have some catching up to do."

"I should say so." He went on to give her an account of his deal with Charley Drake, their one day of work together, Charley's absence, and the incident with Wilson. When he finished telling that part of the recent events, Nora spoke.

"I heard he was here and then left. Do you think he'll be back?"

"I wouldn't be surprised. He left on the northbound stage, so he'll probably come back through. And I think he'd like to get at Aldredge. He just didn't say anything to me."

"I would expect him, then."

"I think so." Fontaine went on with his report of recent doings. He told of Charley Drake's last night, with some hesitation when he came to the part about Charley using Emma to try to get money out of Aldredge.

Nora's eyes were moist, but she held them steady. "Did he say that she actually did the . . . blackmailing?"

"He wasn't that specific, but that was what I gathered. That she delivered the message when she had Aldredge by himself."

"What a cad. On top of everything else, he's out consorting with—"

"I know."

Nora shook her head. "Well, who am I? Men wouldn't pay for those things if women didn't do them, and women wouldn't do them if men weren't willing to pay. Men have always had the power and the money, but women have known how to draw men with a single thread." She shook her head again. "Enough of that. But he actually said she was in on it."

"He said that much. If he had lasted longer I might have gotten more out of him."

After a couple of seconds, Nora said, "The question comes up as to why he didn't silence them both, but the answer comes right with it. They could set Charley up to take the blame."

"And with Charley gone, it's not too hard now to blame him a second time, at least as far as putting out more rumors."

The creek was not far ahead, and they were walking on the vacant side of the street. Nora stopped and gazed out at the distance. "So now the same question comes up. Where does that leave us? We're confident that we know who did these things, but it would be very difficult to prove it. All we've got is hearsay."

"Even if Wilson comes back."

"So do we remain content with what we have, that we got our answer? I don't know. Maybe I haven't let it sink in yet, but I'm not satisfied." She turned to let her eyes meet his.

"Neither am I. Even if Wilson doesn't come back, I feel that I've still got a stake in this thing."

Her eyes searched him. "Go ahead."

"It's bigger than Emma, and it's bigger than Judith Deaver. At the same time, it's all about each of them. And the girl in Kansas."

Nora's head moved in agreement, and her grey eyes were steady. "You mean bringing this man to justice."

"That's right. For the higher idea in general as well as for any of these women in particular. Not to mention Charley Drake and even that poor wretch of a fellow named Ray Toomel."

She resumed walking toward the creek. "Oh, yes. I heard about that. What is there to that story?"

"Well, as you probably heard, Walt McClatchy and I found him dead in Charley Drake's shack."

"And why do you think he ended up that way?"

"I'm not sure, but my guess is that they got as much out of him as they needed."

"You mean in shooting Charley Drake."

"That, and maybe finding something out there in the dirt. Whether he was looking on Aldredge's behalf or looking on his own, he might have found something. Even if he didn't, he knew more than someone else cared for."

"And so the sheriff is in town now, looking into these two occurrences."

"That's what I've heard. I haven't talked to him yet. Mc-

Clatchy has, so I'm sure I won't have much to add. About Toomel, at least. As for Charley's shooting, there were a dozen men closer than I was at the moment."

"And the things Charley told you about Aldredge?"

"I have mixed feelings about how much of that to make public. For right now, at least. It might put me out in the open even more as a person who knows too much. And it would put you there, too, for that matter."

"You say, for right now."

"I'd rather work on something we can prove first."

"Do you mean like—" She was interrupted by a sharp, brief crash of thunder overhead.

"Like finding Judith Deaver," he answered. "Then we can add to it if we want to."

"You think you can find her?"

"I know where Toomel was looking. And if this man Wilson comes back, he can help."

They were close to the creek now, where it curved in an oxbow and the red willows grew up. The air began to move, rustling the willow branches and the reeds and bringing the smell of moisture.

She held out her hand. "There's a raindrop."

"And we're at the farthest point on our walk," he said. "We'd better start back."

Drops began to fall, plopping on the dry ground and rattling on the willow leaves and the rushes. The rain was slanting from the west.

"Let's walk fast," she said. "I don't want to run if I don't have to. Not in these shoes."

He moved to her right side, to shelter her as he could, and he took her hand. Together they hurried along where the rain was wetting the dirt and the buffalo grass. She leaned toward him and held on to his hand.

The rain began to fall harder. "We may have to run," she said.

Wet dirt was starting to spatter up onto the grass, and puddles were forming in the vacant street. A crash of thunder rolled through the clouds above.

She began running, and he kept pace with her. The large, cooling drops fell on his back and his right side, soaking his shirt and wetting his skin. Water ran off the brim of his hat. They reached the corner where they were to turn right, and when they made the turn, the rain came right at their faces. He lowered his head and turned to her. She was covering her brow with her left hand as she held on to him with her right. They kept running.

When they came to the alley, he saw a lean-to ahead on the right. It was a shelter for firewood, and the stack took up less than half of the area.

"Let's duck in here," he said, and he pulled her along.

They came to a stop beneath the overhang. Water flowed off the edge in runnels and splashed six inches high in the dirt and weeds. Fontaine and Nora stood a foot apart, catching their breaths. He let go of her hand and took off his hat to shake it.

As he held it by his side, he looked her over. Her dark hair was plastered to her head and neck, and water dripped off her nose. Her dress was soaked, and it clung to her upper body.

"You're wet," he said.

She laughed. "So are you."

"Well, you said you'd take your chance at getting wet, and this is what you get."

"No harm done. I'm glad I left my hat inside. I was right about that."

"You're not cold, are you?"

"No. Actually, I need to cool down a little, after that run."

"You did all right."

"I had help."

He took her hand again, and she looked at him from below her damp eyebrows. A current hovered in the air, not unlike the energy of the rainstorm, but palpable as well in the touch of her hand. The rain pattered on the roof of the lean-to, ran off in sheets, and splashed like a waterfall. He moved toward her as she did the same. He put his arm around her where the wet dress clung at her waist, and his eyes closed as his lips met hers.

Water sat in puddles in the dished-out areas in the middle of the main street, but the morning air was clean and the sky was blue. The sun had not yet begun to heat the day. Fontaine walked along the sidewalk to the post office, wondering what to expect in his visit with the sheriff.

Inside, Fontaine let his eyes adjust from the bright morning. The sheriff sat at the table where men often gathered to drink coffee and exchange knowledge and opinions. Today the sheriff sat by himself, and there was no coffee pot on the wood-burning stove behind him. Fontaine's first impression was that the sheriff could have been a brother to Doby the bartender, as he, too, had blondish greying hair, a bushy mustache, and a head that hung forward. Unlike the bartender, however, he wore a high-crowned, cream-colored hat, taller in back than in front, and a black leather vest with a lawman's star pinned to it. He had a small sheaf of papers in front of him, and he was reading the top page with his forefinger along the right margin.

He cleared his throat and looked up. "Yes?"

"You're the sheriff?"

"I am. What do you need?"

"My name's Jim Fontaine, sir. I'm a friend of Charley Drake and one of the two men who found Ray Toomel."

"I recognize your name."

"And I was wondering if there was anything I could help you with."

The sheriff's mouth seemed to hang under as he spoke. "You should have a better idea of that than I do."

"I'm not sure what you mean."

"In the matter of Charley Drake, did you hear or see anything different from, or in addition to, the other men present?"

"I don't think so. I'm curious, of course, as to whether you've settled on who did it."

The sheriff made a long face with his mouth closed. "Everyone wants to point to Ray Toomel, but he's become scarce, notwithstanding you and your friend's report."

Fontaine's eyes narrowed. "I don't follow you."

"It's not my custom to give out information that might make things harder for me. But in this case, it's no secret. I went out there with a man from town, and we found nothing. No body, no blood, no signs of a struggle, nothing. No horse either, of course."

Fontaine let out a low breath. "Whew! There was no mistake on our part, and there were two of us."

The sheriff's mustache moved up and down. "All I can say is, there were two of us, and we didn't find anything."

"Just out of curiosity, who did you go with?"

"The barber. We went in his wagon. Thinkin' there would be somethin' to bring back."

Fontaine felt as if he had hit a dead end. "I sure don't know what to say."

The sheriff said nothing, and he did not look at anything in particular.

Fontaine hesitated. He thought he was getting the message that it was time to go. "Well," he said, "if I learn anything else, or find anything else, I guess I'll let you know."

"Sure."

"And I'm sorry if you think we gave you a false report."

"I didn't say that."

"But it must look strange."

"Men do unpredictable things," said the sheriff. "After a few years, things that are strange to other people seem normal to me."

"Do you mean making up stories or moving bodies?"

"I've seen both, and more than once."

After the burial, Fontaine and McClatchy went out to Charley Drake's place for a second time. Inside the shack, Fontaine thought there should be something like a haunted feeling, but all it felt like was a dead man's house.

"It's got me baffled," he said. "If they wanted to hide the body, why didn't they do it to begin with? Unless they were just stashing it here, where someone was bound to show up and find it."

"No tellin'," said McClatchy. "But he sure ain't here now."

"I don't think it was a waste of time to come out here and make sure."

"Oh, no. And while we're at it, we can do what we talked about before."

"What's that?"

McClatchy looked at the floor. He took on an innocent expression as he said, "See if there's anything that can, you know—like you said, something you don't want others to get their hands on."

"My God, we just buried him this morning."

"I'm bein' practical, that's all. We can take care of some of it now, or we can come out again. Tomorrow, next day. Next week."

Fontaine felt his stomach tighten. "I guess there's no difference," he said. "Where should we start?"

"You go first. Take that Dutch oven, for example, and the

skillet. Looks like the lid fits both, and you've got a good iron pothook to go with 'em. You don't have anything like that, do you?"

"Well, no."

"Take 'em, then. Charley would want you to. And that crowbar, too. And here's an ax."

"I've got an ax."

"That's right. We'll put it with the things we'll sell. They've got his horse, his saddle, and his pistol all in town. There should be a rifle around here somewhere."

"I don't know. This just doesn't—"

McClatchy twisted his mouth, then spoke. "Like I said, I'm just bein' practical. Whoever came out before can come out again. Why let 'em steal from him? Besides, if you take something for what you chipped in, I won't feel so bad about takin' somethin' to pay me back."

"All right," said Fontaine. "I guess I'm in the iron business." He found a couple of burlap sacks and wrapped up the skillet, the lid, and the Dutch oven. He set them on the table and laid the pothook and the crowbar next to them.

Meanwhile, McClatchy was rummaging around and muttering. Now he spoke. "I'll be damned. I think they took his rifle already. I shouldn't be surprised."

Fontaine caught the smell of hot metal as he lifted the cast-iron skillet from the fire. He set the skillet on a rock, then swiped a folded rag into the can of bacon grease and came up with a gob. He smeared the grease around the interior iron surface. It melted right away, giving a black shine to the bottom of the pan as the aroma of bacon lifted on the air. Fontaine set the skillet on the fire until wisps of black smoke began to rise, and then he put it on the rock to cool. Next was the Dutch oven, which was wet from scrubbing as the skillet had been. As the fire began to dry the metal, beads of water skittered down the inside and sizzled on the grey bottom. When the kettle was hot and dry, he pulled it from the fire and swabbed it with the rag and bacon grease. As he left it to heat a second time, he wiped the rag on both sides of the heavy lid, then finished with the pothook. It was a good piece of iron in itself, half an inch round and two feet long with a coiled metal handle on one end and a sharp-angled hook on the other.

He set the Dutch oven on the rock to cool as he took the skillet and the pothook inside. He set the skillet upside down on the table and laid the hook next to it. His eyes rested for a couple of seconds on the crowbar that hung on a nail on the wall. These were all good tools, made of iron and steel. They didn't carry much personality with them, and he would put them to good use. Maybe someone else would do the same after he was gone.

He had left the Dutch oven and the lid on the table and was standing in the doorway when he saw Walt McClatchy riding across the grassland on his way from town. It made sense to Fontaine, as McClatchy had gone back in to do his errands while Fontaine lugged his ironware to his own place.

McClatchy rode up to the cabin on a walk and came to a stop. He dismounted and hung onto the reins.

"Any news?" said Fontaine.

McClatchy shook his head. "Nothin' about these two dead men."

"Did you happen to see Barrett and Call?"

"Nope. Word is, they haven't been to town since before Charley and Toomel died. Since the night they had the scrape with that other fella."

"Wilson."

"The roughneck."

"Any news of him?"

"Nah. They're afraid he'll come back to town and tear up someone else. They're glad the sheriff's in town."

"Who's afraid?"

"Well, I wouldn't say everyone. I heard it from Glenmore."

"Who's he?"

McClatchy tipped his head and twisted his mouth to one side. "You'd know him as a friend of Doby, the bartender's. Fat man."

"Wears a dark suit?"

"That's him."

"They're pals of Aldredge, aren't they? Anyone else would have been glad to see Barrett and Call get taken down a notch."

"I think he likes to stay in good with Gus."

"Stool pigeon. He was the one who went for Aldredge the night Charley got killed. What does he do, anyway?"

"He owns a few buildings and rents 'em out. They say he made a lot of money in fish."

"In fish?"

"Yeah. He had a fish market in Omaha. He sold it and came out here when the land deals were going strong."

"No wonder they're pals." From the way McClatchy moved his lips and averted his eyes, Fontaine guessed that he and Glenmore were on easy speaking terms. So Fontaine changed the subject. "When would be a good time to go after those poles? Like you said, it would be just as well not to leave 'em lying around."

"Tomorrow would be all right."

"How shall we meet up?"

McClatchy narrowed his eyes in thought. "Here's the best way. You leave your horse at my place, we get the poles, leave 'em off here, and you ride back with me to get your horse."

"Wouldn't it be shorter for me if I met you there at the creek and rode back?"

"Not really. It's shorter to my place than it is to there."

"But all together, it's longer if I have to ride to your place and back. Unless you want me to ride in the wagon with you."

"Well, we have to go across some of Gus's place on the way there."

"I think his men would be less likely to give you trouble if I wasn't along. They don't have anything against you, do they?"

McClatchy's eyes shifted. "I don't know. After all, I was the one that reported Toomel, and you and I were in on it together. If he wasn't goin' to be there that long, we'd have been better off if we'd never found him."

"You think they did it, then? I do."

"I just know the sheriff has asked 'em plenty of questions, and I suppose they're not happy about it."

"Oh, well. I'll ride with you. The drive won't seem like so much if you've got someone to talk to."

The trip to the creek the next morning went without incident. McClatchy kept the horses hitched so he could move the wagon from one stack of poles to another, and the two men had everything loaded in a little more than an hour.

"Not bad," said McClatchy. He gave his self-satisfied smile. "I thought we could get that many in one load. If you want, we can throw on a few pieces of dry stuff so you'll have some firewood."

They found a scattering of deadfall where a tree that looked something like an elm had died and fallen over. The tree looked like better fuel than cottonwood, so they used McClatchy's ax to trim off the smaller stuff and then tossed a half-dozen dead, bent branches on top of the load of straight poles. With the sun not yet at its high point, they rolled out of the cottonwood grove.

On the way back to Fontaine's place, McClatchy took the

route that Charley had taken the day he and Fontaine had come together. It went past the homestead of Adam and Al, which Fontaine had gone around when he traveled by himself.

"Couple of boys startin' their own place," said McClatchy. "We'll see how they're doin'." He drove the wagon around the left of a low hill, down into a low spot and up again, then down again into the broader swale that Fontaine recognized.

As they drew close to the site, Fontaine noted the progress the men had made. The dirt they had been scraping on that earlier day had been dark, and now the mound on either side of the excavation was topped with whitish-tan loose clay. The men's bearded faces were visible above the mound, and for a moment they reminded Fontaine of prairie dogs.

McClatchy brought the team to a halt at the front of the hole. He called out, "Hullo, boys. Findin' any buried treasure?"

"None here," said Adam.

"Buildin' a dugout?"

"Root cellar."

"Pretty similar, with the front open like that."

Adam took in the load in the wagon. "Got yourselves some poles, huh?"

McClatchy pointed with his thumb. "They're for him."

Adam lifted his head in greeting. "Sure. We've met. How are you doing?"

"All right," said Fontaine. "We left you plenty of thick poles."

"That's good. We'll be ready for 'em pretty soon."

McClatchy proceeded to ask Adam a series of questions about the length, width, depth, and roof height of the project. Then he asked how they were going to do the sidewalls, the front, and the door. When he had gotten answers to all of his questions, he said, "What you need is some rocks."

"Biggest ones we've dug up here are about an inch across.

Even at the creek, you won't find any bigger than six or eight inches."

"Lots of 'em up in the buttes," said McClatchy. "As big as you can lift onto your wagon."

Adam glanced to the west. "I don't like to go there."

"We're goin'. Get some cedar posts." McClatchy turned to Fontaine. "Isn't that right?"

"It's an idea. One step at a time. I might as well get all of my poles first."

Adam turned to hear something from his brother. Back to McClatchy, he said, "You want some antelope meat? Al shot one a couple of days ago, and we won't be able to eat the whole thing before it spoils."

McClatchy said, "Make some jerky out of it."

"Even if we had time, we've still got more than we need." Adam looked across at Fontaine. "You'll take some, won't you?"

"Is it all right? Not spoiled?"

"You'll want to eat it in the next day or two." Adam climbed up out of the hole, and his brother went back to swinging the pick. Adam went into the tent and came out with a lump wrapped in newspaper. "This is a hindquarter," he said. "All meat, no bones. You can split it between you."

"Thanks," said McClatchy. He took the bundle and set it on the floorboard.

"Well, I'd better get back to work," Adam said. "Thanks for stoppin' by."

"You bet." McClatchy lingered. "You're going to cover the roof with dirt, then?"

"That's right. Poles, then boards, then canvas, then dirt."

McClatchy nodded. "That should do it all right."

"We think so." Adam turned again toward his work.

"Well, good enough," said McClatchy. He spoke to the horses, and the wagon began to roll.

They had gotten back out on the rail and had gone about half a mile when two riders appeared from out of a draw that slanted from the southwest. Fontaine's stomach tightened as he recognized Barrett and Call.

The two riders hit a lope and came up behind the wagon on the left. As they came close, they began to holler, "Yee-hah! Yee-hah! Wha-ha-ha!"

As they thundered past, the wagon horses broke into a run. McClatchy planted his feet and pulled back on the reins, but the horses kept running and the wagon began to sway. The two right wheels lifted from the ground, and some of the firewood and top poles fell off. McClatchy kept pulling on the reins and hollering "Whoa!" until he brought the wagon to a stop.

He sat still and said, "Let 'em cool down."

Fontaine looked back to see the dead, crooked limbs lying on the trail. The poles had rolled into the sagebrush so that only a couple of cut ends and a few patches of bark were visible.

"We'll go back and get 'em," said McClatchy.

After a couple of minutes he turned the wagon around and headed back to the spilled pieces. About a dozen poles had rolled off along a stretch of fifty yards, so the men loaded them first and then threw the dry limbs on top.

The rest of the trip was uneventful, and the unloading did not take long.

"Let's go ahead and divide that antelope meat," Fontaine said.

McClatchy wrinkled his nose. "I don't really care for any."

"I can't eat it all myself."

McClatchy looked at the sun. "Well, give some to me, then. I've got to go into town. Maybe I can give it to someone there."

Fontaine rode to McClatchy's place with him, and by the time he got home he was plenty hungry. He built a fire, sliced some antelope meat, and fried it in his skillet with bacon grease.

When he was done eating and had things cleaned up, he went to work on the firewood. He was glad he had an ax, because most of the wood was too thick to break.

The sun was going down when he finished with the firewood. He left it in a pile and put the ax away. As he stood in the doorway and looked out on the lengthening shadows, he saw McClatchy coming back from town.

When he stopped his horse, McClatchy acted as if they had spoken just a few minutes earlier. With an expression that raised his cheeks and made his eyes squint, he said, "I been thinkin'. If it's all the same to you, I think it might be better if you cut all your poles first. Then we go for the posts. Maybe the weather 'll be cooler then."

"Sure. Whatever works best. I've got plenty to do. At some point I've got to peel all these as well." Fontaine recalled the harassment from earlier in the day. "Did you see Aldredge's men in town? They looked as if they might be headed that way."

McClatchy shook his head. "Didn't see 'em. Heard one thing that might be interestin', though." He waited a couple of seconds for effect, and then he said, "That roughneck fella named Wilson came back to town."

CHAPTER THIRTEEN

Fontaine looked first in the Pale Horse Saloon, thinking that Wilson might avoid the Old Clem out of dislike for the bartender. Only two men stood at the bar of the Pale Horse, however, and neither of them was Wilson. They were engaged in conversation with the heavyset bartender, and all three looked at him as if he were an intruder. He turned around and went out.

The Old Clem Saloon had half a dozen men along the bar and one man seated by himself at a table. Fontaine recognized the bullet-shaped hat, trimmed mustache, and hard-featured, sallow face of Harold Wilson. He had a whiskey glass in front of him and was rolling a cigarette. As he licked the seam, his eyes came up and gave Fontaine a look of recognition.

Fontaine took a couple of steps to reach the edge of the table across from Wilson. "Mind if I sit down?"

"Go ahead." Wilson stuck the cigarette in the side of his mouth and lit it.

"Glad to see you came back to town."

Wilson shook out his match. "I needed to go up to Lusk. Fella up there owed me some money, so I figured I could kill two birds with one stone on this trip."

Fontaine let the silence hang in the air for a minute until he spoke. "Did you know Charley Drake?"

"The fella that just got killed? I heard of him."

Fontaine glanced around and wondered how sociable Wilson

had been in the Old Clem. "Did you hear about him in here?"

Wilson blew smoke out through his nostrils. "I heard about him gettin' killed when I was up in Lusk. But I heard of him before that. He looked up the woman that knew Judith. She told me his name."

"Is that how he knew about Penfield and Pomeroy, or did knowing about them lead him to her?"

Wilson leveled his hard brown eyes on Fontaine. "Mister, I don't know what he knew or how he learned it. But he got himself killed."

Fontaine kept his voice low. "And he may have gotten this other girl killed as well. Or helped her on the way."

"That's their lookout. Or was." Wilson drank down the last quarter-inch of whiskey in his glass.

"What I was gettin' around to was, or is, that I've got an even stronger hunch than before that the same person is behind these things."

"You've got your stake in it, and I've got mine."

"As far as that goes, I want to see him brought to justice for everything he's done." Fontaine looked around to be sure no one had come within earshot. "The girl here, your friend Judith, the girl in Kansas, even Charley Drake."

"I'd leave that little son of a bitch out of it. But that's up to you."

"Did he do something I don't know about?"

Wilson looked down his nose at the cigarette he held near his mouth. "Sidles up to a woman to try to get somethin' for himself. Lets on like he was an old friend of Judith's and wanted to set things right. Well, he used 'em both, and prob'ly this girl too, and you see where it got him."

"Then he knew Judith's name."

"Of course he did."

"He told me he didn't."

"I'm sure he told a lot of people a lot of things." Wilson took a long pull on his cigarette and let the cloud drift up around his face.

After a few seconds Fontaine said, "Have you had anything to eat?"

"Not since I got to town. Last time I ate was this mornin'."

"What would you think if we went somewhere to get a bite to eat? I'll stand for it."

Wilson looked at his empty glass. "That would be all right." He rose from his chair and cupped the last of his cigarette with his left hand.

Outside, Fontaine paused on the sidewalk. "Let's try that café at the station. I think it might be pretty quiet."

Wilson took a last drag on his cigarette, smoking it down to his fingertips, and dropped it on the sidewalk where he ground it out. "Let's have another drink first," he said.

They crossed the street and went down the block to the Pale Horse Saloon. The same two men stood at the bar. The heavy-set bartender with the broad forehead and beak-shaped nose came to wait on them.

"Glass of whiskey," said Wilson.

"I'll have the same." Fontaine laid a silver dollar on the bar.

Wilson waited for his drink, took a sip, and brought out his tobacco. He rolled a cigarette at his own leisure, ignoring Fontaine as he had done before. He leaned on the bar, and still without speaking he smoked his cigarette and drank from his glass. When he was done with his cigarette, he dropped it on the floor in front of him, looked down, and stepped on it. The door opened and he stood up, his right hand near his trousers pocket. He stayed standing up when the man passed behind him, and he continued to drink with his left hand.

The bartender reappeared with the bottle in his hand. "Have another?"

"Might as well," said Wilson.

Fontaine said, "I've still got some." He pointed at the silver dollar that sat on the bar. "Take 'em all out of that."

"Will do." The bartender poured another slug of whiskey in Wilson's glass, covered the silver dollar with a hand that worked like a cat's paw, and glided away.

Wilson drank his second whiskey a little faster than the first one. When he was close to the bottom, the bartender came back and paused with the bottle in his hand but did not say anything.

Wilson looked at him and spoke. "Is that other place the only one in town that has a card game?"

"The Old Clem? Yep."

"I guess they have girls sometimes, too."

"They've got everything. Fistfights and shootings, too." The bartender stood with the bottle poised. "What all are you lookin' for?"

"None of it." Wilson tossed off the remainder of his drink. "We're goin' to get somethin' to eat."

The bartender set the bottle on the shelf behind the bar and leaned forward to collect the glasses. "Thanks for stoppin' in."

"A pleasure," said Wilson.

The café at the stagecoach station was unoccupied except for the pale young man with the premature baldness. He slid off the stool where he had been leaning against the back wall with his eyes closed. He stood for a second and opened his eyes wide, then came forward.

"Sit anywhere," he said.

Fontaine moved to the table where he had sat before, against the left wall. He and Wilson sat across from one another, each with a view of the window and door. Fontaine looked up at the thin young man.

"Have you got any steaks in the kitchen?"

The waiter gave two quick nods. "Oh, yes."

"I'd like a steak with some fried potatoes."

Wilson said, "I'll have the same."

The young man's eyes flickered. "It'll be a few minutes. I'm the only one here at this time of day."

"That's fine," said Fontaine. "We're not in a big rush."

Within a minute, sounds came from pots clanging on a stove. Fontaine decided to re-open the subject.

"I've tried to imagine the place you told me about, but it's not very clear. You said it was a spot where a draw came down between two hills, but like you said at the time, there's a dozen places that all look like that."

"You said there was someone out there pokin' around?"

"That's right. He's dead now, too, as it turns out, but I know where he was probing with an iron rod." When he saw that he had Wilson's interest, Fontaine went on. "It's a big, wide country once you get out there, but the area that Aldredge has tried to get his hands on is a little over a square mile, about a section and a half. That's where my place is, and that's where this fellow was pokin' in the ground."

Wilson had his hands together on the table in front of him, and he moved his thumbs as he spoke. "Sure. They knew where they were goin', at least in general. But it was at night, and there weren't any landmarks right there, like a tree or a rock or whatever. But accordin' to Pomeroy, it was a place where a draw came east between two hills and sort of leveled out. You could see it from a half-mile away, and in the moonlight, with the two hills and the flat area, it looked like a woman's body. That's what he said." Wilson's hands moved, and he glanced around the small café. "I wouldn't mind a drink," he said.

"We'll get one after we leave here." Fontaine paused for a couple of seconds and returned to the topic. "Anyway, so they wouldn't go back out there, and whoever did was unable to find it."

"Yeah."

Fontaine frowned. "Even if things look different in the daytime, you'd think they could find a mound of dirt."

"I guess they did a good job. Scattered the extra dirt and put the grass right-side-up." Wilson took out his tobacco sack but did not open it. "It'll sink over a period of time, but not like if you buried a horse or something like that. If you're lookin' for somethin' at this point, I'd say you should look where the ground has sunk in, not where it's mounded up. Just my idea."

Fontaine could see that Wilson was not letting sentimentality get in the way at this point, so he said, "The ground won't pack down that hard by itself in a couple of years, and you would feel an iron rod come up against something like a bone, so this fellow might have found something if he was in the right place. But when I saw him, he was pokin' where the dirt was mounded."

"Oh, I'm not sayin' he was wrong. And if he's dead, maybe he found something."

"But that shouldn't keep us from trying."

"Not at all," said Wilson. "If they found something, the game's up and we don't know it. But if they haven't found anything, and we run into 'em, we might be able to tell it." Wilson shifted in his seat and put his tobacco back into his pocket. He scowled in the direction of the kitchen. "What the hell's takin' him so long? You'd think he had to kill the cow."

"It shouldn't be long. Sounds like he's frying the spuds now. We'll eat good, then go have another drink."

Within a couple of minutes, the pale young man came out of the kitchen with two oval platters of fried food. He set them down and went to sit on his stool.

"Back to this other thing," said Fontaine as they cut into their steaks. "I think it's worth a try. What would you think of starting in the morning?"

Wilson made a backward motion with his hand. "Sounds fine."

"Good. I can get us another horse. You ride all right?"

Wilson gave him a level gaze with his brown eyes. "Oh, yeah. Don't worry about me."

Fontaine met Wilson as agreed at the livery stable at seven in the morning. When Fontaine had left him the evening before in his usual pose of smoking a cigarette and brooding over a glass of whiskey, he wondered how alert the man would be in the morning. As he stood now in the shadow of the front of the livery stable, Wilson was not only on his feet but clear-eyed, and with his hard demeanor he seemed steeled for any encounter.

Fontaine adjusted the stirrups, and Wilson climbed aboard. He had not brought food, water, a jacket, a sidearm, or anything a person might carry along for a day's ride. He just got on and was ready to go. He evened his reins and walked the horse in a circle out in the street, then waited as Fontaine got mounted. They rode out of town with the sun at their backs.

The horses moved at a fast walk in the cool of morning. The buckskin, being used to the route, plucked right along in the direction of the home place. The livery stable horse kept pace alongside, on Fontaine's right. Wilson did not speak for the whole five miles, but he kept his head up and his eyes moving.

"We're on my property now," said Fontaine.

Wilson nodded and moved his head from side to side, as if he was taking a new look.

A few minutes later, Fontaine said, "I thought we could go to the spot where I saw that fellow probing. We'll stop and get a shovel first."

Wilson made no expression in response, but he gave his horse loose rein and let it move along with Fontaine's as the trail veered toward the cabin.

The buckskin let out a long snuffle and a blow when they came to a stop in Fontaine's dooryard. Wilson got down and walked around, leading his horse, as Fontaine went for the shovel and tied it on.

"Do you need anything?" he asked.

Wilson shook his head. "Not now."

They mounted up and rode west up the gentle slope until they came to the edge of Fontaine's property. There they turned right and rode toward the hill where Fontaine had witnessed the strange, silent scene of Ray Toomel poking into the barrow of earth. Before they reached the crest, Fontaine stopped and dismounted so that he could move up the hill a little at a time and not barge into sight all at once. Wilson followed his example.

As the draw came into view, it looked different in the morning light than it had in the dusk of evening. The draw was a broad area, almost flat, with a scattering of low sagebrush. As Fontaine looked at it anew, he thought it could match the description Wilson had given the day before. His eyes roved until he found the spot where Toomel had been making his motions. It, too, appeared to have changed.

"It's over there," said Fontaine. "It looks as if someone's been digging."

He led his horse downslope to the flat area and moved toward the uneven pile of dirt. "We're onto Aldredge's property right now," he said. "It's a quarter-section like mine, and he got it from a fellow he persuaded to sell out. Name of Welch. One thought is that he bought it because it might be where Penfield and Pomeroy did their buryin'."

Wilson's bullet-head hat went up and down as he nodded with interest. He walked straight for the site of the disturbed dirt and got there a step ahead of Fontaine. He pushed on his reins to make the horse step back and away.

Fontaine moved forward and got a look for himself. Someone

had dug a hole about a foot wide, a foot deep, and four feet long, tossing the dirt to either side without much of an attempt to keep it in a neat pile for shoveling back in.

"Dead end," said Wilson. "They hit solid dirt."

"Looks like it. We can check for ourselves." Fontaine handed his reins to Wilson, went to the back of his saddle, and untied the shovel. Without much worry that he would find something serious, he went to the edge of the hole and began stabbing the shovel head into the hard earth at the bottom of the small excavation. "Seems pretty solid. As you can see, this was mounded before. Who knows why. Maybe gophers at some point. But I don't think there's been a hole filled in down here."

Wilson had his lips pushed out and was shaking his head. "I didn't think so."

"Well, it was the most obvious place, so it was worth looking at." He stepped back and held the shovel upright with the head resting on the ground.

The sound of hooves on dry earth made them both look up. Two riders had come over the hill from the southwest and were headed down the slope toward Fontaine and Wilson. They were familiar enough that Fontaine recognized them in the first instant.

"Look who's here," he said. He reached out and took the reins of his horse from Wilson.

Barrett and Call kept riding at a lope and came to an abrupt stop on the other side of the dug-up area. A drift of air carried the smell of dust, dry grass, and sweaty horses.

Barrett raised his head and gave a critical glance downward at Fontaine's shovel. "What the hell do you think you're doing?"

"Not much."

"You know you're on someone else's land."

"That doesn't seem to stop you when you're out and about."

Fontaine looked at Call. "Like you say, you need to fence it out."

Barrett's voice cut the air. "Goin' across someone's land is one thing. Diggin' on it's another." He leaned forward with his forearm on the saddle horn, and his blue eyes bore down on Fontaine. "You don't do that. It's like walkin' into a man's house and goin' through his cupboards."

Fontaine thought, *Like someone did to Charley Drake.* But he had no proof. "I'm not digging," he said. "I'm lookin' where someone else dug."

Barrett spit tobacco juice to the side. "You make me laugh. You carry a shovel onto another man's land, I see you diggin' in the dirt, and you have the gall to deny it."

"I wasn't digging. I was seeing how solid the ground was. Laugh all you want, but any fool can see that this dirt wasn't dug up this morning."

Barrett's neck seemed to disappear as he hunched forward to bear down again. "Don't call me a fool."

Wilson's voice came out steady. "Maybe he didn't."

Barrett shifted to stare at Wilson. "Maybe you want to."

"I don't have to."

Silence hung in the air for a long second until Barrett's mouth curled into a thin smile and he said, "It's good to see you out here where no one can interfere. We can finish what we started the other night. And keep your hand out of your pocket or I'll put a bullet through you."

Barrett dismounted, and as he was uphill, he did not look as short as he sometimes did. He handed his reins to Call, who had also dismounted and had come up behind him. Then he took off his hat and handed it to Call as well. Sunlight fell on the white inlets of his receding hairline, on his short-cropped hair, and on the scar that ran across the top of his head.

Wilson was calm as he took off his hat, hung it on the saddle horn, and handed his reins to Fontaine. "Take off your gun and knife," he said.

"To keep things fair? You make me laugh just like he does. But sure, I'll take 'em off." Barrett unbuckled his gunbelt and handed it to Call without looking at him. He slipped the sheath knife off his trousers belt and put the belt back in place. Then he leaned his head forward, pulled his shoulders up and inward, and tightened his eyes so that they glared. An aura of animal-like hostility emanated from him, and he had the appearance of a strange beast—part man, part prehistoric bird, and part fighting animal, like a badger. With a tight smile he said, "Ready."

Call and Fontaine each held a pair of horses as the two fighters moved onto an open area uphill from the dug-up spot. Wilson, lean and jailhouse-tough, had his fists at chest level, while Barrett, compact and beast-like, held his a little lower. They each circled to the left until the animal lunged. Wilson blocked the punch and hit his opponent a glancing blow on the side of the head. Barrett straightened up and got back into position. He smiled and made a waving motion with his left hand.

"C'mon, c'mon."

Wilson stepped forward and landed a left to the jaw. The round-muscled man came right back with two fast punches that rocked Wilson's head and lifted it so that the wine-colored birthmark on his neck came into view.

Wilson backed off, made a cautious study, and moved forward. He drew a punch from the shorter man and leaned back so that Barrett's fist caught only air. Wilson peered at his opponent, swayed back and forth, feinted, and hit him in the nose.

Barrett put up his hand, flat, but no blood came away. He smiled again and leaned forward with his shoulders hunched. Now he made a series of attempts at lunging forward and driving his fist through Wilson's guard. On his fourth try, he dropped lower and drove at the man's waist.

Wilson sprawled back, pushing Barrett's head down with one hand and punching it with the other. The compact man held on like a badger, got a hold of Wilson's leg, and lifted it. They danced for a second in clumsy motion until Wilson hit the beast with a sideways uppercut and Barrett pushed back, causing him to fall on the ground. Wilson scrambled up, and Barrett regained his footing with just enough time to kick his man in the ribs.

"That was hardly fair," said Wilson as he finished standing up.

"Every fight is fair." Barrett, still hunched, moved his foot as if he were going to kick again, and Wilson flinched. The short man laughed.

Wilson went back at it in serious fistfight style, and he succeeded in hammering the brute's temples with a series of three punches.

Barrett came back with his head lowered and his arms windmilling. His fists glanced off of Wilson's skull and cheekbone, and once again he dropped down to grab his opponent by a leg. He came up on the side, lifted Wilson's leg over his own thigh, and reached from behind to grab the man in the groin. As Wilson went up on tiptoe, his antagonist drove forward and smashed him onto the ground.

Wilson jerked his elbow back and hit Barrett in the teeth, then bucked him off and got away. As he came to his feet and had his left side to the fight, he reached into the off-side pocket of his trousers.

Barrett, who was halfway up, rose with a surge. He lunged at Wilson, locking his arms around him and pinning his right arm to his side. Then he picked up the man, balanced him for a split second on his hip, and slammed him to the ground. Barrett showed tremendous energy and rage as he jumped on his enemy, straddled his chest, and landed one blow after another on the man's face. Wilson bucked and twisted and flailed, but the animal hung on. He had his left hand like a claw on Wilson's nose, then twisted his ear, then dug his fingernails into the cheek below Wilson's eye, all the time hammering with his right fist.

Barrett shifted position, got both hands on the man's throat, and got up onto his knees so he could put more weight onto his hands. Wilson's right hand was loose and he was swinging upward, but the man on top had his head tucked in, and the punches were swinging around and bouncing off.

Barrett forced down with his left hand on Wilson's throat and smashed him five times with his right fist. The man on the bottom seemed to be losing resistance, but the horrid bundle of fury on top was not slowing down. He got both hands on Wilson's throat again and slammed his head to the ground a dozen times until the body went limp.

The creature that looked like a crouched beast began to expand into human form. He took deep, bristling breaths as he pushed back, rose in a crouch, and crawled off his victim. He stood up, then bent over and reached into Wilson's pocket. He drew out a brass bar about four inches long and three-quarters of an inch in diameter. He held it out for the other two men to see, then let it drop on the dead man's abdomen and roll onto the ground. He threw back his head, opened his mouth, and said, "Hah! He took me at my word, by God! But he wasn't good enough."

Call cleared his throat but didn't say anything.

"Every fight's a fair fight, and he believed it, too." Barrett's chest rose and fell as he pulled in air to speak. "Go report this to your sheriff. I'll be glad to talk to him." The short man, still with a trace of grotesqueness, breathed in through his open mouth. "I beat him, by God, fair and square, man to man." His voice had a quaver in it, and his hand was shaking as he took his sheath knife from Call and put it back on his belt, but there was no question about how exultant he felt. He took his hat and put it on, then buckled on his gunbelt with deft movement. He licked his lips like a thirsty man, took the reins from Call, and whipped up into the saddle. He took one last look downward at Fontaine and said, "Man to man. Any son of a bitch that wants it."

The two henchmen rode away, leaving Fontaine in a daze. He felt washed out by the dread and, he realized, by the hopelessness of standing by and watching such an act. He looked at Wilson, and although there was no question about the outcome, he found it difficult to believe that a man who was as hard as the rock wall of a prison was now dead as a stone.

CHAPTER FOURTEEN

The bacon crackled and sizzled in the cast-iron skillet. Fontaine sat on one of the thicker cottonwood poles and gazed at the coals of the outdoor fire. The whole prospect of getting a new start on his own little piece of ground had become disheartening. Aldredge and his men had ridden roughshod over everything, intimidating and beating and killing anyone who posed a threat. McClatchy had not come around, but he had no doubt heard about Wilson by now. The sheriff had taken it as a matter of course, saying that it sounded like a fair fight that turned out unlucky for one side. All the same, he would talk to Barrett.

Then there was the dream. After taking Wilson's body to town and talking with the sheriff, Fontaine had come home, eaten the last of the antelope meat, and gone to bed exhausted. At about one or two in the morning, he had the nightmare. Maybe it was the meat, which had begun to turn yellow as antelope meat did in warm weather. He had heard that meat gave men bad dreams. More likely, he thought, it was the aftereffect of seeing what Barrett had done.

In the dream, Fontaine was riding across the range. The grass was high. As he rode, he saw that he was in the midst of a vast graveyard. His horse was loping, and every second or third time the horse's feet touched the ground, hands reached up from the graves. They were live hands, not skeletons, the hands of the dead who would not stay dead. The ground opened up, and the hands reached, grasping for his stirrups and the bottoms of his cinches. He saw faces he did not recognize, he heard voices that did not speak words, and always he saw the hands that wanted to pull him down. He called out indistinct, ineffective words, and his own shouting woke him. He was alone, in his cabin, with a feeling of revulsion in his stomach.

He was not able to go back to sleep. He waited out the rest of the night—or morning—until grey daylight came to the rangeland again. Then he got up and tried to make a normal day of it.

Maybe it was the meat. He still felt sick to his stomach. The first couple of sips of coffee hadn't made him feel any better. He hoped the bacon would. He had two cold biscuits to go along with it.

After his five-minute breakfast he poured the bacon grease in its can, wiped out the skillet, and left it upside down on the table inside. He boiled another cup of coffee and sat on the cottonwood pole to drink it. When things went still and quiet like this, he expected McClatchy to come along, but he remembered the man's evasive tone in their last conversation, and he figured McClatchy would keep himself scarce until things blew over.

Fontaine drank the last of his coffee and shook out the grounds. He was almost out of water, and his horse needed a drink. With nothing else pressing, he could go to the creek.

Fontaine was using the crowbar to hammer loose nails on the cabin when he saw a rider approaching from the direction of town. The horse was not moving very fast, so he went back to hammering in order to finish the side he was working on. The rider was still not close enough to identify. Fontaine took the crowbar inside and hung it on its nail. He hadn't thought much of it when he first got it, as it was only about two feet long and not very heavy, but it was handy for smaller work.

Fontaine put on his gunbelt, checked the loads in his pistol, and set his rifle by the doorway. The rider was too small to be McClatchy and too slight to be Barrett. Fontaine had not seen the sheriff on horseback, but he expected the sheriff would have more of a slumped posture and would be wearing his cream-colored hat with the tall crown. Fontaine could not tell what kind of a hat this rider was wearing.

A couple of minutes later, he saw why the rider was hard to identify. It was a woman. Fontaine stepped out into plain view, and Nora waved. He took off his hat and waved it to her.

She was riding a small bay horse with a lightweight saddle, and she was wearing trousers and a grey cotton work shirt. On her head she had a short-brimmed, flat-crowned woman's hat of dark blue felt. As she rode up to the cabin she smiled, show-ing her pretty teeth, and she raised her hand to wave again.

"Shall I help you down?" he asked.

"I can manage." She brought the little bay to a stop, grabbed the saddle horn, lifted her near foot from the stirrup as she drew the other foot over the saddle, and slid to the ground. With another smile she said, "I might need help getting back on, though."

"My horse is out on picket. If you'd like, I can tie this one to that dead tree over there. Do you plan to be here for more than a couple of minutes?"

"I'm in no hurry. I asked for the day off."

"Let me do that, then, and we can go inside. It's still cooler in there than it is out here, though it warms up later in the day. Did anyone follow you?"

"Not that I noticed, but I kept most of my attention on this fellow."

Fontaine patted the bay on the nose. "I've seen him in the stable. He seems gentle enough."

"He treated me well."

Inside the cabin, he brushed off one of the two rickety chairs and set it in the middle of the room for her. He pulled the other one around for himself. When they were both seated, he sensed that she was waiting for him to speak, so he did.

"I was surprised to see you come out here on your own."

"I was worried. I heard about what happened yesterday, and I was troubled that I didn't get a chance to hear from you. Though I could understand why you might not have been in a mood for visiting."

"I'll tell you. I was in a daze. It was an unsettling thing to witness. Sickening, really."

"You brought the body in, I understand."

"It was the one thing I felt at least capable of, though it was no small task in itself."

"And the sheriff? Didn't he see this as one more move in a whole pattern?"

"I think he saw it as a continuation of a feud. And when two men have it out like that, with no weapons, it's hard to say that one party came in and killed another, although that was the end result."

Nora frowned. "What were you doing when it happened? I heard that the two of you were digging on Aldredge's land."

"We were looking for Judith Deaver. We went to a spot where I had seen Ray Toomel probing with his iron rod, and it was on Aldredge's land. We found where someone had been digging there, but we didn't find evidence of anything having been buried, much less dug up. That's as far as we got when those other two showed up. Barrett had a grudge to settle. Wilson was a hard man, but Barrett has a streak that's—I don't know, very foul, and it runs deep. It was as if he had this vile animal down inside of him and it came out, stronger than any person." Fontaine shook his head. "It was hard to believe, but I saw it. And he gloated in such a terrible way afterwards. I don't know

201

if you've ever caught the strong smell of a snake, but it works its way into you and can make you sick to your stomach. And I did get sick, through my whole body, and I had a nightmare. I ate the last of some antelope meat that was on the verge of spoiling, and that might not have helped, but it was this other thing, I'm sure. As far as the effect on my body, it was worse than a bad fall from a horse. And I've had a couple of those that have left me shaken, especially once when the horse went wild and I couldn't get loose."

Nora's grey eyes searched him. "I'm sorry it happened, which I know is a small thing to say. And I'm sorry for this man Wilson, though I didn't know him."

"He might have been crooked in some ways, but he came here to get justice for a woman he cared about. He wasn't sentimental, and he despised someone feeling sorry for him, but all the same, it was a bad way for him to go."

She looked at her hands, together in her lap, and then up at him. "And so we're back to our old question again. Where does it leave us?"

He held his breath to keep from letting out a weary sigh. "I don't know. I feel like I'm all on my own. Even Walt McClatchy is keeping his distance." His eyes met hers. "But we can't just quit, I know that. We can't walk away and let someone get away with these things. Like we said before, these people deserve justice—especially Emma, but Judith as well, and the girl in Kansas whose name we don't even know. And, to some extent, Charley Drake and Harold Wilson, though they brought some of the trouble on themselves, and even Ray Toomel."

"I'm still reluctant to admit it about my own sister, but perhaps Emma, like Judith, brought some of it on herself. But it doesn't give a man like Aldredge a right to—snuff them out like a candle."

Fontaine waited for her to say more, and when she didn't, he went on. "And even if we did walk away at this point, there's no guarantee we'd be left alone. Unless we went far away. But I don't feel like giving up this little piece of land I've just gotten started on, just because someone thinks I know too much."

"And you're pretty sure they've got you placed that way?"

"I don't see how they couldn't, when you consider the ones I kept company with."

"You think they know who Wilson is—or was?"

"If I could find out, they could. Even Charley Drake probably knew, though he kept things to himself. Penfield and Pomeroy, for example—he knew they were dead. And he knew Judith Deaver's name even though he told me he didn't."

"So when we speak of people who are a little bit crooked, he's one of them."

"And one among several who knew too much." Fontaine let his eyes rove over her. "That's a quaint outfit," he said. "It makes you look innocent."

"Like an orphan or a waif?"

"Something like that. Seriously, though, if you got out right now, you could stay in the clear."

She set her face in an expression that was both firm and playful. "I thank you for the compliment on my outfit, which I chose with great care from the closet of left-behind clothes at The Gables, but I don't plan to leave just yet."

"Well, I think there's trouble in store for both of us unless we can get someone locked up."

"And your idea of how to do it?"

He smiled. "I'll tell you, your visit has cheered me up and made me feel a little more competent. As for my idea, it's the one I had before. We go out and find Judith Deaver." Nora's eyes widened, and he made a quick addition. "When I say *we*, I don't mean to assume you have to go along."

Her eyes remained wide, and he realized she was looking past him. He turned to see George Call standing in the doorway with his walnut-handled pistol leveled at both of them. His hat was tipped back, and his red kerchief hung loose around his neck. His waxy nose and jutting ears looked all the more prominent as a smile broadened his face. When he spoke, his sarcasm was as heavy as a cow's breath.

"When I say *we*, I mean a couple of things. To begin with, why don't *we* put our gun over there on the table. With your left hand. Then *we* stand in back of her, and be careful. If I have to shoot, I might hit her instead of you. Or both of you at once. So be careful. *We* don't want to make a mistake."

Call stepped into the cabin and kept them both covered with his six-gun. Fontaine saw that he had gone past the rifle leaning by the doorway and must not have seen it. As Fontaine set the pistol on the table, his hand came within a couple of inches of the skillet handle, but he didn't think he could wield the heavy object fast enough to do any good.

Call waved his gun. As Fontaine moved toward the chairs, Call stepped sideways to lay his left hand on Fontaine's pistol. Nora must have caught sight of the rifle, which was in clear view now. Call followed her eyes. With a pistol in each hand, he backed over toward the rifle. He had taken off his jingle-bob spurs, so none of his steps made much noise.

"Too many guns," he said as he worked Fontaine's pistol into his waistband in back.

Nora stood up. "Then give me one," she said.

"Sit down."

She took a step forward, blocking Call's view. As she did, Fontaine laid his hand backwards on the crowbar where it hung on the wall.

"Sit down, little sister, and don't get hurt." Call grabbed the front of her shirt, but the result was delayed because of the looseness of the garment, and his left fist came back to his shoulder while she pulled her head away. He tried to swing her to the left and then to the right, and she stumbled in front of his gun hand.

The movement gave Fontaine the opening he needed. He came around on Call's left, bringing the crowbar up, over, and down on the base of his skull beneath his ear.

Call fell like a stunned steer, and Nora scrambled away. Fontaine's arm was shaking as he stood over the man. Call had covered his pistol when he fell, and Fontaine didn't know if he was going to have to hit the man again. He was ready to.

He leaned forward and pulled his own pistol free. After putting it in his holster, he leaned again and felt for a pulse on Call's neck. Nothing.

Fontaine stood up. His heart was beating fast, and his mouth was dry. With the crowbar still in his hand, he went to the doorway and searched the landscape. Looking over his shoulder, he said, "He must have come by himself, following you." He looked at the body slumped on the floor. "High hopes."

"Is he—?"

"He's done for."

"I'll tell you, I'm not sorry a bit."

"Neither am I, but sooner or later his pal will come looking for him." Fontaine gazed out again at the country.

"What do you think we should do?"

Fontaine had a sensation of clear thought and vision. "Stash him at Charley Drake's, and go looking for Judith Deaver."

They left Call's body inside the shack where Ray Toomel's body had been for a short while, and they left the horse in the pen outside. Earlier, at the cabin, Fontaine had kept the pistol with the walnut grips and put it in his saddlebag. He took it out now and showed it to Nora.

"Remember where this is in case you need it. Here's how it

works." He pointed the gun away from both of them. "The hammer's on an empty chamber right now. You click it back into place like this, aim it with the hammer and this sight, and pull the trigger." He eased the hammer down, clicked the cylinder into its proper place, and stowed the gun in the saddlebag.

"I hope I don't have to," she said.

"So do I. Because if it gets that far—well, just remember where it is."

"I will."

"Good. Now let's get out of here." He boosted her into the saddle, swung onto his own, and got into motion.

He struck a course that he thought would bring them close to the spot where the southeast corner of Charley's land met the northwest corner of his own. He kept an eye out for the small pile of rocks he had placed as a boundary marker, and in a short while he found the place. The rocks were no longer in a pile, though.

He drew his horse to a stop and swung down. "I had these rocks in a stack," he said, leaning over to pick one up, "to mark the corner of my property." He moved the reins to his left hand and picked up another rock. "But someone scattered them."

Nora slid down from her saddle and led the bay horse a few yards away to pick up a stone. She knelt as she picked it up. "Peevish on their part, isn't it?"

"Yes, it is." He began to build the base with the larger rocks. She handed him the stone she held, then turned and knelt to pick up another. He was amused at her delicacy of not bending over in front of him.

When they had the marker rebuilt, she led her horse away and stopped him in position. "I'm ready."

They had already been through the method a couple of times, so he didn't need to say anything. He stood by the stirrup, held his hands palm up, and locked his fingers. He bent over so that his joined hands were at the height of his knees. She grabbed the saddle horn and lifted her foot into his makeshift stirrup, and in a smooth motion he boosted her up and gave her thigh a nudge with his shoulder.

She settled into place and smiled down at him. "You're getting good at that. I might have to keep you around."

The side of his face still felt a tingle from brushing against the leg of her trousers, but he held his hands up, locked again, and said, "It's all in the motion. There's hardly any weight to lift."

She smiled again. "Don't you know the right thing to say."

He mounted up, and they rode on. They were on his property now. They crossed a low hill, and he looked back to his right where a shallow draw angled from the west. He stopped his horse.

"What is it?"

"Looks like more digging." He reined his horse around, and Nora moved up alongside. "See that spot behind the sagebrush? It looks like a pile of dirt."

"Whose property is it?"

Fontaine thought for a second. "The same as the other place I told you about, where Toomel had been poking around and then someone did some digging. It belongs to Aldredge. He bought it from a man named Welch, pushed him out, not long after Judith disappeared."

Fontaine rode forward, and Nora kept up. At the mound of exposed dirt, he could see that whoever was digging hadn't gone far. "Same thing," he said. "They dig a little ways, and they see that the dirt's the same as it's been for ages." He raised his head and looked around at the landscape. "It's a big country to find one little hidden place."

Nora motioned with her head toward the shovel he had tied

onto his saddle. "Do you not need to dig, then?"

"Not here. I can tell from looking."

They turned their horses, and as they headed downslope toward Fontaine's parcel, Nora spoke again. "Do you think they've been looking all this time? You'd think they would have found her."

"I think they've had an eye out all this time, but it seems as if they started pressing when Charley Drake made his move and let them, or Aldredge, know that someone was onto him. At about the same time, I settled on my place, and that seems to have got them going, too." He glanced around and said, "We're back on my land now."

"Do you think she's here?"

"I have a hunch she is, if only because they've been looking on this other place, which is so close, and haven't found anything. What I think I need to do is look at things from a different angle, or different approach, than I have before. So I think we'll go this way."

They followed the draw they were in until it widened out to flat range. Fontaine estimated that they were somewhere in the middle of his property, so he made a wide turn and headed west again, toward the buttes. He brought the buckskin to a stop, and Nora drew up on his right on the little bay.

"Up ahead," he said, pointing, "A little more than a quarter of a mile, is the first place I told you about, where they poked and dug and didn't find anything."

Nora shaded her eyes and nodded. "That's where you had the trouble."

"Right." The buckskin shifted, and when it was still again, Fontaine said, "From back here, the landscape looks exactly as Wilson said Pomeroy described it—two hills and a draw that levels out. But Aldredge's men, or Toomel by himself, were looking for places where the earth was mounded up or seemed to be. Wilson's idea, and I agree, was to look for a place where it's been sunken in."

Nora's grey eyes held steady on him. "From the decomposing. But what about the extra dirt?"

"Wilson said they put the sod back in place right-side-up and scattered the loose dirt. One season of rain would make that hard to see."

"Shall we go on foot?"

"I suppose we could. Things are that much closer to look at." He dismounted, then watched as she did the same.

They led their horses and meandered along. Fontaine studied the ground and kicked an irregular tuft of grass here and there.

Nora's voice came on the thin air. "What do you think of this?" She had stopped at the edge of a small depression.

Fontaine walked over to join her. "Could be. You know, it doesn't take much at all for weeds to get a start, and it looks as if there might be a seam here and here." He pointed at two little rows of foreign plants that broke the carpet of native grass. He stood back. "It's about the right size. It's laid out east and west, and all this time I imagined it north and south. That's how those other places are dug up, as far as that goes. But these fellows were digging in the moonlight and looking at the buttes, so they could have done it either way." He surveyed the length again. "It's worth a try."

He untied the shovel and handed the reins to Nora. Then he paused at the edge of the area where he planned to dig. He pointed the head of the shovel at the west end.

"If she's here, I would bet her head is this way. But if it's the other way—I'll start in the middle, that's what."

The ground was hard, even where he thought he found a seam. He cut out chunks of sod almost three inches thick, with the familiar black roots sticking out like hairs, and he set the pieces in order on the south side of the hole. When he had an area opened up about three feet square, he began to dig down.

"The dirt is looser here," he said, "but that's not unusual underneath the sod. Here's something, though."

Nora moved closer, holding both sets of reins, and the horses edged up with her.

Fontaine continued. "If the dirt's never been disturbed, it's all the same. At least on its level. You don't have to dig down very far, sometimes a foot and sometimes less, to get to a new layer and see a different color. You can look at the side of your hole and see the changes. Here the topsoil is dark, then you get a tan clay, and after that a kind of white clay. All in a couple of feet or less. When someone fills a hole back in, that dirt gets mixed. That's what it looks like here." He dug and stabbed and carved and scooped until he had a hole about a foot deep. The dirt did not come out in separate colors but, as he had said, mixed.

He stood back to take a breather, and he realized his heartbeat had picked up and his arms had a nervous energy coursing through them. "I think we might be onto something," he said. "This dirt's coming out like I said, and even though it's been packed, it's not as hard as the little bit of digging I've done around the cabin."

"And if we find her?"

"I don't think we want to dig it all up and disturb the evidence. Just enough to be sure, and then turn it over to the sheriff. Even if someone comes along, they'll play hell—excuse my language—getting it all dug up and moved before the sheriff can get back out here. It's not like moving Ray Toomel all in one piece." He pushed up from leaning on the shovel. "I guess I'd better get back at it."

"What shall I do? I can help dig. You're perspiring already."

"It's not that hard, and we've got but one shovel. Just hold onto the horses, and try not to faint if you see something morbid."

"I'll look the other way."

"Good plan. I think I'll make the hole a little longer and then go down. I would bet they didn't dig more than three feet deep altogether."

He did as he said, and as he dug out a new wall at each end of his excavation, he saw again that the dirt was not in layers of separate colors. It came out one shovelful after another, some of it caked and some of it loose, and the mound grew on the north side of the hole.

He was down about two feet now, and he had to climb into the hole for the next part. He stood with his back to the east, hoping he was not standing on someone's upper body, and he began scraping sideways with the blade of the shovel. He was deep enough that he did not want to be jabbing the point and hitting something human.

He scraped and scooped and tossed the dirt out in small amounts now. The sun had crossed into afternoon, and he was sweating in the trapped heat and dust of the open pit.

The edge of his shovel caught a new resistance. It was not dirt, or a pebble, or the deepest root of sagebrush. It dragged and then gave no more, and the shovel turned. He scraped again, and the shovel skimmed over. He scraped again, and it caught. He scraped each way, and a ridge of wrinkled dark cloth showed in the dirt.

"I found something," he said.

Nora stepped to the edge of the hole behind him. "Fabric."

"So far. But you might want to stay ready to look away." He bent and began to scrape away more dirt. After a dozen passes, he uncovered enough of the tattered garment to know what it was. "A woman's dress," he said, pointing his shovel. "Here's where it was gathered at the waist, this part is the skirt, and there's the upper part." He raised his glance to the far edge of the depression. "Like I thought, they buried her with her head to the west."

He rested with one hand on the shovel. He was thirsty, and his lips were dusty. Sweat was running off his forehead.

"The poor woman," said Nora.

Fontaine took a deep breath and used the shovel to push himself up out of the pit. He stabbed the shovel into the mound of dirt, tipped back his hat, and dragged his cuff across his brow. "I think that's as far as we need to go right now."

A voice from in back of them sent a jolt to his stomach.

"I'd say so. Now turn around slow, both of you."

Fontaine knew the voice, and he turned to see the short-necked man with a narrow-brimmed hat and liquid blue eyes. Barrett was holding an ivory-handled pistol, and his sheath knife was on his left hip.

He spit to the side, and his lower lip came back moist. "I thought I might find George out here, but it looks like I did a lot better than that."

CHAPTER FIFTEEN

Barrett held his gun steady as he stood with his feet planted and his hips forward. His mouth curled in a short smile as he spoke. "Get off to the side, Miss Puss, and you, puncher, throw your gun in the hole." When Fontaine did not move right away, Barrett's voice turned menacing. "I said throw your gun in the hole, or I'll put a hole in you bigger'n a Chinaman's peter. Don't look shocked, Miss Puss. I'm sure you've seen a couple peters in your life, and you might get to see at least one more before long." His blue eyes came back to Fontaine, and his trigger finger moved. "The gun, puncher."

Fontaine lifted his six-gun by the handle and dropped it into the hole. It thudded in the dirt, and he knew he wouldn't want to try to fire it even if he could get his hands on it.

"Man to man," said Barrett. He put his left thumb in his belt, near the front, and seemed again to be leading with his hips. "Man to woman. Everything a fella could want. A little more to the side, Miss Puss."

Barrett's eyes held on Fontaine. "You don't like me talkin' that way, do you? Well, let's do something about it." He put the gun in his holster and began to walk forward.

Nora was crowding the horses and pushing them away. Fontaine could barely see her because the buckskin was in the way. She had her back to the grave and her right side to Barrett, and she was fussing with the reins on the bay. She pulled the horse around to stand between her and the man who was moving closer.

Barrett stopped within eight feet of Fontaine and drew his knife with his right hand. He tossed it to his left, then back to his right. "You've seen this knife before, haven't you?" He tossed it in the air and let the handle drop flat into his palm. "There's something I didn't tell you about it." He flipped it, caught it by the blade, and held it up by the tip. "This handle is made out of the thigh bone of a man." He tossed it again so that the handle fell into his hand. He curled a nostril. "I made him my woman. No, that's a joke. But he would have done it if he thought it would save his life." Barrett peeked around the head of the bay and leered at Nora. "Maybe that's a joke, too. Maybe I just found it, diggin' around for bones like some people do." He turned his liquid blue eyes toward Fontaine. "When they shouldn't."

Barrett shifted his left foot and widened his stance. He flipped the knife again and caught it by the handle. "Here's the deal," he said. "I can stick this in you wherever I want and whenever I want. And then I can do what I want with Miss Puss." He flipped the knife, caught it by the blade, and leaned the handle toward Fontaine. "Unless you're man enough to take it." He flipped the knife again, snagged it with his left hand, and drew his gun with his right. He smiled and put the gun back in its holster, then tossed the knife over to his right hand.

Fontaine kept his eyes on Barrett. He thought Nora was moving toward the saddlebag, and he didn't want to give her away. He was sure he had left the bag unbuckled so that someone could get to the gun fast. To draw Barrett's attention, he said, "Did you give Ray Toomel that much of a chance?"

Barrett made a dry spit and said, "Huh."

"Or Charley Drake?"

Barrett wrinkled his nose.

"Or Emma?"

Barrett's eyebrows tightened, as if Fontaine had hit too close to home, but he shifted his eyes instead of answering.

Fontaine's heart almost stopped when Barrett said, "Get over here, Miss Puss."

She backed up, turning the horses inward.

"I said get over here. Let those horses go."

She turned the buckskin the rest of the way so that its hip was toward Fontaine. "What for?" she asked.

"Because I said so. Maybe I want to cut your buttons off."

She gave the buckskin a shove so that it backed up. Fontaine moved to the saddlebag, reached in, and got his hand on the gun as Barrett came forward and reached across with his left hand to slap the horse on the rump. The look on Barrett's face changed from annoyance to surprise when he saw the .45 pointed at his midsection. He dropped the bone-handled knife and clawed at his six-gun as Fontaine pulled the trigger. His arms flung out and his hat fell away as he snapped backwards.

The horses stampeded with a thunder of hooves. Nora took slow, cautious steps forward and kept her eye on the man on the ground.

Fontaine saw that the horses had joined up about fifty yards away. He turned back to Nora. "Thanks for the help," he said.

"I was more than glad to. I thought you had a better chance at it than I did."

"I was worried for a while, but it turned out all right." Fontaine recalled the look on Barrett's face when he slapped the horse out of the way. "He was surprised. In a regular gunfight, you're supposed to give each other a chance to draw. But we were way past that."

"I should say so. He made you throw yours away."

"Like I heard him say more than once, every fight's a fair fight. He just couldn't believe that someone else might come out on top."

★ ★ ★ ★ ★

The sheriff did not look up from his papers right away when Fontaine walked into the post office. He was dressed as usual with his cream-colored hat, taller in back than in front, and his black leather vest with a lawman's star. His head hung forward, and his bushy mustache made small movements as he followed his reading with his forefinger along the right margin. The page was handwritten, and when he reached the end of a paragraph he looked up.

"What do you want?" he asked.

"I was wondering if you found everything all right."

The mustache moved as if he was preparing his words, and then he spoke. "You people have kept me plenty busy. I've been wanting to leave this town for days. But, yes, this time there was a dead body in the shack where you said it was, another one out on the prairie staring at the sky, and a more advanced one down in the hole."

Fontaine's pulse picked up. "And the one that was buried. Was there enough to identify something?"

The sheriff's face lengthened as his eyebrows went up and his chin went down. "The first two were easy to identify because I had talked to each of them in the recent past." The sheriff blew out a breath. "I don't know what the score is because I haven't found Ray Toomel and I don't know whose side he was on, but I'd say you've evened it. For the time being, at least, I'm takin' your lady-friend's word that you acted in self-defense."

"If I hadn't, you'd be—"

"We'll leave it at that. It's hard enough for me to know what happened, much less what might have happened."

Fontaine glanced at the handwritten page, which would have been hard to read even if it were right-side-up. "And the person who was buried?"

"From the clothing we could say it was a woman. She had a

leg bone that had been broken and then mended at some time in the past, and she had a bullet hole in the head."

A shiver ran through Fontaine's neck and shoulders. "Then it matched what I said."

"We didn't find anything with her name on it."

"But the mended bone—"

"That will be a help. It'll take time, but we'll probably be able to put a name on those remains. As for who did it, or why, I can't say how far we can get with that."

"Well, the two men who did it are dead, and so are the two who told me what I know."

"What you think you know. After all, it's just what you heard."

Fontaine made himself take a breath. "And what about the man behind it—behind this woman's death and the one we know happened in this town?"

"Your lady-friend's sister."

Fontaine's spirits sank as he heard the sheriff mention it in such a casual way. "Yes. What about—Aldredge?"

"I can't find him. He seems to have left town."

"When?"

"I'm not sure. I asked him some questions after I talked to you and Miss Winterborne yesterday, and when the barber and I got back from rounding up our bounty, he was nowhere to be found."

"How did he leave?"

"Quickly and quietly, I would say."

"In his buggy? On horseback? On the stage?"

The sheriff's mouth tightened, and then he spoke. "For someone in your circumstances, you're throwin' yourself around quite a bit here. If anyone's goin' to ask questions, it'll be me."

Fontaine settled into his boots. "Very well. Do you have any questions for me?"

"Yes. Don't you have somethin' else to do?"

Fontaine walked out and stood in the bright sunlight. He told himself to stay calm. The fat was in the fire now. Aldredge knew that his two bullies were gone, and if he hadn't heard it from the sheriff he would have heard from someone else that Nora was Emma's sister. He had to be at his last ditch, and it would be natural for him to try to get away. If Fontaine knew how he had left, there might be a way of running him down and bringing him to justice.

He walked across the street diagonally, staying wide of the Old Clem, and went into the livery stable. The interior of the building had not heated up yet, and the sweet smell of hay drifted on the air. The stable man came out of the harness room carrying a broom with a head as curved as a horse's tail.

"What do you need today?"

"Nothing in the way of horses. Just information. Do you know if Aldredge has left town?"

"I wouldn't know, but his buggy's in the shed, and his horses are in their pen." The stable man waved the broom toward the open back door. The two palominos stood with their heads over the top rail of a pen.

"I see. And you didn't rent him a saddle horse?"

"Oh, no. He hardly ever rides."

"Thanks. I appreciate it."

"Any time."

Fontaine walked out of the stable, crossed the street, and turned north. Within a few minutes he had his hand on the doorknob of the stagecoach station café. Resisting the temptation to look across the street at Aldredge's house, he turned the handle and went in.

The pale young man came out of the kitchen and stopped. "Oh, hello," he said.

"What's the matter?"

"Nothing, I guess." His eyes flickered. "I heard you'd been in some trouble."

Fontaine smiled. "I'm not going to cause any in here unless someone comes out of the kitchen pointing a gun at me. Then I might run like hell."

The young man remained humorless. "There's no one else here."

"Do you work this place night and day?"

"Pretty much. If they ever pay me, I want to get out of here and get back to my wife."

"You told me that before. Where is she?"

"With her folks in Minneapolis."

Fontaine was beginning to hear a slur or lisp that he had heard in the young man before. "How did you end up here?" he asked.

"I went to look for work in Seattle. It didn't turn out, and I went broke before I could get all the way back." His eyes stayed in one place, though they were a little closer together than on some people. "This is a terrible place to get stuck in."

"I believe it." Fontaine handed him a quarter. "Maybe this'll help."

"Thanks."

"Don't mention it. But tell me the truth, the best that you can remember. When was the last time you saw Mr. Aldredge?"

The young man blinked. "I don't know."

"You know who he is, don't you?"

"Sure. He lives over there."

"He didn't leave on the stage yesterday or today, did he?"

"No. I don't think I've ever seen him on the stage. He has his own whippy, you know. Comes and goes in that."

"I've seen it." Fontaine's mind skipped to the next point. "What do you know about the Old Clem Saloon?"

"I stay away from those places. Both a man and a woman have been killed there since I've been in town."

"Who owns it?"

"I think Mr. Glenmore owns the building. He owns this one, too."

"And the business? Of the saloon, that is?"

The young man shook his head. "I don't know. You'd have to ask."

"I might." Fontaine held out his hand. "Thanks, pal. I hope you get back to your wife."

"So do I."

Fontaine went outside and walked back the way he came. He crossed the street to the livery stable and went around back. The shiny tan buckboard was parked in the shed, and the palominos were still in their pen. Several other horses stood in pens as well, among them the little bay horse that Nora had ridden and the brown one Fontaine had rented for Wilson. Dust was beginning to rise as horses moved in their pens, stamped, and swished their tails. Other than that, not much was going on.

Fontaine walked down the alley. In back of a house on his left, white and red hollyhocks were blooming at three-quarters of the way up the stalks. He turned in behind the Old Clem Saloon and walked in through the back door.

A large, dark form lurched in surprise. As Fontaine's eyes adjusted to the dim interior, he recognized the portly man in the dark suit. The name played in his mind. *Glenmore.* Fontaine walked past him and stood at the bar halfway to the front door.

Glenmore's gravelly voice carried in the quiet barroom. "Don't know if they're servin' yet today."

"No one on duty?"

"He's around."

Fontaine stood in silence, listening. He thought he heard the tread of someone coming up a set of stairs, and a moment later he saw Doby behind the bar where no one had been when

Fontaine came in. Glenmore was gazing off in the distance.

"Place isn't open yet," said the bartender.

"I didn't know that. The door was open, so I came in."

"The front door's closed. You'll have to go out the way you came in."

"I'll do that." Fontaine headed for the back door, but when he was even with Doby and Glenmore he stopped. "Do you have rats in your cellar?" he asked.

"Who says I have a cellar?"

"Your feet. I thought maybe you were down there spreadin' rat poison."

Doby faced him with his head hanging forward and a sullen expression on his face. "Mister, you've been nothin' but trouble since the first night you came in here. You don't need to come back."

"That's fine. I'll send the sheriff. Maybe he can find out what you put in people's drinks. Or what you have in the cellar."

Fontaine walked out to the alley and studied the building from each side. A stone foundation ran all the way around, and he could see no windows or storm door. The cellar, as he envisioned it, would be set in a few feet from the foundation all the way around. There was a possibility of a tunnel, but the next place north was the little saddle and harness shop, and the next place south was the coal and drayage company. So it looked like one way in and one way out, which, according to the old saying, not even a rat got himself into. Then again, the Old Clem Saloon had two doors.

Fontaine went around by way of the drayage company, passing between the buildings, and crossed the street to the post office. It was closed. He went to the barber shop, and it was closed, too. He walked around to the alley, where he found an old man sitting in the shade of an overhang in back of the post office. Fontaine recognized him as the postmaster. He had a crusty loaf of bread in his lap and a quart jar of beer by his foot. He was working his mouth up and down, and as he didn't have many teeth, his lips moved in and out, and his mouth smacked. A wad of dough disappeared, and he spoke.

"Lookin' for the sheriff again?"

"That I am."

"Well, they had to go to Lusk. They couldn't ship that woman's remains on the stage, so they had to do it by train. They left just a little while ago, him 'n' the barber."

"I see. I guess it'll have to wait."

"Damn few things that can't. Anyone bleedin'?"

"Not that I know of."

The old man tore off a hunk of bread. "Then I'd come back tomorrow. They won't get back till late tonight."

"Thanks." Fontaine walked north to the end of the alley, turned right, and followed the cross street beyond the main drag and to the back of the livery stable again. As he turned into the alley, an object showed through a small cloud of dust ahead. It was a covered tan buggy drawn by two palomino horses.

Fontaine broke into a run. The buckboard was moving faster than he could run in his boots, and he wondered if he could catch it. Then it stopped—in back of the Inland Sea Café—and a man in a light-colored hat and suit jumped down. Aldredge himself. As the man hurried to the back door, Fontaine wondered whether Gertie was in cahoots as well.

His question was answered when Aldredge reappeared dragging Nora by the arm with one hand and swinging his pistol at Gertie with the other. Nora pulled back, then swung with her left hand and knocked off Aldredge's hat. Gertie was grabbing onto his gun hand, but he pulled loose and hit her in the face with his elbow. She dropped to a sitting position as he swung his free hand, and with the pistol barrel pointing upward, he struck Nora in the face. Then he picked her up with both hands, threw her under the canvas hood of the carriage, and jumped in.

Fontaine got there in time to lay his hand on the tailboard of the buggy. It pulled him faster than he could run, his steps going way out in front of him and then way behind, until he lost his grip and fell face forward in the dirt. The palomino horses charged into the street, yanked the buggy around to the left, and disappeared from Fontaine's view.

He scrambled to his feet and wiped his face. He could never catch that thing on foot, not now. Where was his horse?

In front of the post office.

He turned and took off on a dash.

As he ran, he thought, Aldredge had to be a fool to think he could get away. But he had Nora as a hostage, and he knew who she was. This was his last ditch.

Fontaine cut between the drayage company and the saloon once again and saw the post office straight ahead across the street. But his horse wasn't there.

As he burst out onto the sidewalk and got a view of the rest of the street, he saw his horse walking toward the livery stable. It was being led by a portly man in a dark suit.

Fontaine had a new burst of energy as he changed direction and ran down the middle of the street. Glenmore turned at the sound, showed surprise in his face, and started to run with the reins still in his hand. Fontaine caught him before he went far. Glenmore dropped the reins and put up his hands palm outward, but Fontaine charged through and knocked him down. He wanted to hit the man a few more times for laying his hand on the horse, but time was wasting. Fontaine grabbed the reins, slapped them into place, and vaulted into the saddle.

Around the corner and down two blocks, Fontaine came out at the edge of town. The buckboard had not gone as far as he thought it might, though it was boiling up a cloud of dust as it went past the oxbow where the red willows grew.

Fontaine spurred the buckskin and began to gain ground. He could not see either Aldredge or Nora through the covering, but the vehicle was on a steady roll. Fontaine lowered his head and kept riding. He thought he could catch the buggy, but he didn't know what he would do when he got there. If he did anything to spill the vehicle at this speed, Nora could get hurt or killed. He needed to stop it, and then he had to deal with Aldredge.

The idea occurred to him that he might be able to rope one of the horses. That would make him less vulnerable than riding up and grabbing it. He had his rope tied on as always, though he hadn't done anything but drag firewood with it for a while. He took it down and shook out a loop. As he came up on the left side of the buggy, he saw how close he was going to have to get, and he realized he would put himself in Aldredge's line of fire after all. But he could veer aside or drop back. He gauged his chances and decided he had to try it.

The palominos had settled into a lope that was not top speed, and for all Fontaine knew, Aldredge was not aware of how close he was. He spurred the buckskin, swung his rope three times, and made his throw.

The rope fell dead on the horse's back and bounced off. From the corner of his eye, Fontaine saw Aldredge rise in his seat and point a six-gun. Fontaine sagged back as the shot whistled by. He dropped his rope and pulled his six-gun.

Aldredge, half-risen in a crouch and hatless with his hair riffling, grabbed the frame of the awning with his left hand as he turned and pointed the pistol with his right. Fontaine held on him dead center and fired.

Aldredge hunched over, raised his gun, then dropped it and pitched over the side. The buckskin jumped to the left as

Aldredge hit the rim of the wheel, twisted, and fell on the ground.

The palominos had broken into a faster run. Fontaine spurred the buckskin and caught up little by little. A quarter of a mile beyond where Aldredge fell in the dust, Fontaine got his hand on a headstall and brought the team to a stop.

Nora came out the front door of the lodging house with a valise in each hand as Fontaine tied the reins of his horse to the hitching rail.

"A time comes for everything." She set the bags down. "For those of us who get to choose."

He let the bags sit there. "I'm sorry to see you go, but like you say, you accomplished what you came for."

"I don't like the emphasis on my having done it. Very little of this could I have done by myself. But, yes, I saw my sister through it, so I've put that to rest. And with all of this done, you can go back to what you came for."

"Things change."

"How do you mean?"

"If you'd like, I can tie your bags onto the saddle, and we can walk to the station that way."

She moved the bags to the edge of the sidewalk. "I've got plenty of time. If we're going to carry them that way, we can take the long way around."

"By the creek?"

"Yes. You know I like that walk."

He tied the bags on, and they started on their way. Neither of them spoke until they reached the edge of town and turned north toward the creek.

"You left a question unanswered," she said.

"What was that?"

"I asked what you meant when you said things change. You're

not planning to quit here, are you?"

"Oh, no. What I meant was, what I came for isn't exactly the same as I want now."

Her eyes showed interest. "You wanted to make a new start. I remember you saying that. More than once."

"Yes, and you said you wanted to do something similar yourself."

"That's true."

"And you're going back to North Platte, and I'm staying here."

"I hardly think you'd like it in North Platte."

"I'm not much for working in a haberdashery." They walked on for a couple of moments until he spoke again. "You're just making me come right out and say it, aren't you?"

"My stage leaves in a little while, and I don't want to have regrets about things left unsaid."

"All right. What I want now is to make a new start but not by myself."

She smiled. "You choked it right out, didn't you?"

"Well, yes, I did." He felt a tension he wasn't sure of. "And how about you?"

"How about what?"

"I suppose I have to choke that out, too. What do you plan to do in North Platte?"

"I don't have a plan."

"You mean you don't, how shall I say this, assume you have to stay there?"

Her eyes met his, and she shook her head. "No, I don't."

The tension faded. "Whew," he said. "It took a while to get to that."

"It's because you're supposed to take the initiative."

"Like this?" He took her hand, and they walked a few steps until he turned her. "And this?"

"Yes," she said.

And he took her in his arms at the edge of the creek where the water rippled and the red willows grew.

ABOUT THE AUTHOR

John D. Nesbitt lives in the plains country of Wyoming, where he teaches English and Spanish at Eastern Wyoming College. He writes western, contemporary, mystery, and retro/noir fiction as well as nonfiction and poetry. John has won many awards for his work, including two awards from the Wyoming State Historical Society (for fiction), two awards from Wyoming Writers for encouragement of other writers and service to the organization, two Wyoming Arts Council literary fellowships (one for fiction, one for nonfiction), and three Spur awards from Western Writers of America. His most recent books are *Thorns on the Rose,* a collection of western poetry, and *Dark Prairie,* a frontier mystery.